The Scapegoat

JOAN LAWRENCE

The Scapegoat

A Life of Moses

PETER OWEN · LONDON

ISBN 0 7206 0708 6

PETER OWEN PUBLISHERS
73 Kenway Road London SW5 0RE

First published in Great Britain 1988
© Joan Lawrence 1988

Typeset by Ann Buchan (Typesetters) Shepperton Middlesex
Printed in Great Britain by
Redwood Burn Limited Trowbridge Wiltshire

For
Queenie and Humphrey Weber
and
in memory of
Anne

Preface

When we hear the name Moses, we tend to conjure up a larger-than-life figure, remote from today's problems and thus almost inaccessible to our modern sympathies. We know, most of us, the main facts of his life. Although the man himself is hidden by his own myth: leader, prophet, lawgiver, austerely and majestically driving his people out of slavery and across the desert towards the Promised Land. He is indeed a towering 'hero' figure; one of the great men of history whose influence is still active in the affairs of mankind. But that is not all of him. Certainly it is difficult to look behind the confusing threads of biblical narrative; but if we do so, extricating him from the power and authority of his mission, he becomes a warm and engaging human being, even in his undoubted isolation. We find a man of divided emotions, at times a timid man, hampered by his own fragmented upbringing, a man wracked by self-doubt and given to fierce explosions of rage and acts of cruelty. But we recognise, above all, a man of great intelligence, compassion and perception, pulled inexorably between his ungrateful and intractable people and his demanding and arbitrary God. With one exception, he struggled always to convey God's teaching, even if he was sometimes uncertain whether it was his own voice rather than God's which thundered down upon his people.

It is this complex and very human Moses, plagued by his own inner conflicts, which this book seeks to discover: not in any way to diminish the myth but rather to reveal, and so enlarge, the man.

The story, partly inspired by the Rembrandt portrait, is based upon the Revised Version of the Old Testament (the Hebrew Bible). Choices have necessarily had to be made between conflicting accounts. For instance, the crucial episode at the waters of Meribah has been placed as given in the Book of Numbers: that is, following the arrival at Kadesh-barnea, where it has more significance than at any earlier stage of the journey. Again, Deuteronomy has been followed in the use of the name Horeb, rather than Sinai, for the mountain before which Moses saw the burning bush and upon which he received the tablets of the Law, scholars even now disagreeing about the exact name and location.

Finally, it is only to be expected that such a charismatic leader would attract a great volume of legend and rabbinic story over centuries. Save in two instances, these have been ignored, since they would have conflicted with the better-known pattern of the bibilical narrative. One of these exceptions is the reputed power of Moses to see into the future; the other is the legend of his death, which so clearly sums up the sharp contradictions of his life.

Joan Lawrence

Contents

Prologue

They will set horns upon my head, like a goat. But there could be justice in this, for I have frequently been both stubborn and thick-witted. They will also, and zealously, recognise those horns as marks of the evil one, so that my people will inevitably become known as the Devil's children. It will, of course, have been only a regrettable error – this they will decide later – merely to mistranslate with that prejudicial word what my people actually saw: the rays of light, fanning out from my forehead. They may even try to put the matter right. Not that it will make any the less unfortunate that earlier and so dreadful misconception.

But now, before the mistake has been made, I can remember, as if it were yesterday, how my people cowered before me when I came down the mountainside bearing the tablets. Afterwards, they told me that the very skin of my countenance had shone – blazing, it seemed, with a glory, so that they were afraid. I, naturally, was unable to see this. It was my hands, rather, which I could not fail to notice – streams of colour, flaring from fingertips, enfolding the testimony with power. But these my people did not see. Only I. And still I ask myself, hesitating, did the power arise within me? From myself? Surely it came solely from the Lord? Nothing to do with me. His servant. I must be clear about that. Only the bearer. Surely?

Perhaps it would have given consolation had I never become aware of these thrusting horns – and of their menace for my people. Indeed, they lay far into the future. That I knew. Part, they were, of a flickering reality which occasionally came pushing through to claim my reluctant attention. For I never wished to have the future forced upon me, yet often it would simply be there – sudden, vividly glimpsed, as with a curtain twitched aside; aspects of a distant way of living. Mostly, it was a future quite unlike anything I had known, and therefore I was unable to interpret it.

Only the horns were unmistakable, sprouting from my head. Yet I can recall one man who showed me as I truly am, so that I recognised myself with rueful self-disgust. Here, in his creation, is to be seen no angered majesty, no marbled chill of despotism. Just a shadowy darkness and the tablets raised for the breaking. No glory, no shining. Only my large, ungainly body. My face not frowning, but pale and melancholy and somewhat haunted, as if drained by a vision that had been too much to bear.

And now I am old – perhaps even a little childish (I have heard this said of me, however reverently). I am placed at last upon this ultimate mountain, looking out, from the height of eagles, across the Land. It is exactly as the Lord did tell me. Not as Egypt, and not as the wilderness, but green with brooks of water and little fountains springing from the hills. Indeed, it will offer us bread without stinting.

'Us'? No. For me, the river below, winding through the bright meadows, will bar my way, implacably, witness to the Lord's displeasure. I shall remain here, as it was arranged. But without rebellion. Even, now, without bitterness.

For it is strange, after all the journeying years, to discover that my heart remains within the wilderness. Those desert places which we so often cursed, and where our spirit faltered and our faith diminished as a drop of water sinking into sand, have become a part of my bones, so that I should feel bereft and uneasy in the comfort now spread before me.

I am sustained, not by the glittering fall of water, or by the green, luxuriant herbs, but rather by my awareness that far back along the rim of the world I still can see the desert, crouching in the south, sullen and copper-coloured, with its violet shadows and the glare of its uncompromising sun, hungry for my escaping people. It is there as a dull stain under the hard sky, ferocious, unyielding, a trap for the unwary, as exacting as the Lord himself who led us through its wastes.

It was the wilderness which helped to shape us. To make, and also to break. That I recognised, with humility. And now, forbidden as I am to venture into this Land, I am whelmed with relief that I may rest within sight, still, of my appallingly unendurable foe, clinging with gratitude as to an ancient enemy, grown familiar and bringing now the ease of reconciliation.

It will be said of me later, that when I was brought to this place, my eyes were not yet dim and my strength not abated. Yet as I look out, following my commander's ecstatic pointing, my eyes do not see the substance. Instead, I can make out another world impressed upon the one over which my people are rejoicing, a world that ebbs and flows, shifting and disconnected. Oh, certainly it is the Land which the Lord has sworn to us. Yet also there is an unrelated city, outside this present time, set like a lodestar in the far distance.

Curious, that while I yearn towards it, my sight blurred as to its location, I am unerringly aware of each strange detail of its singular construction – aware, too, of what is certainly inconceivable: its teeming, thrusting and extraordinary people. It is, of course, an impossible city. Quite unlike any of those places described to us by the earlier scouts sent into the Land.

But there it is – beginning now to fade a little but conferring on me (so that it pulls at my frail body) the sudden vision of a Wall, to touch which I passionately crave, anguished by an inconsolable longing.

Do you see the City? I ask of Joshua, pointing in my turn. Do you see it? There! The City of David! There, in the distance! And the Wall! The *Wall*. Do you not see the Wall of Yerushalayim?

David? I can tell that he is puzzled, frowning and laughing at the same time. He gently takes my hand. No city, he explains. Perhaps it is a mirage that you see. For even Jebus is away beyond the desert's fringe.

He notes my tears, the easy tears of age, my childish, ancient disappointment. Yet it is true (and he nods eagerly, placatingly) that we shall build you cities. And your people shall inherit them. And both the cities and the people will remember you. For you are our foundation.

I struggle to shake my head. The Lord only is the foundation. Yet he just goes on smiling at me. With love, it seems. Yes, with love. Strange that at last he can accept me.

So I must be content. I remember in my confusion, as I feel

Joshua's arms supporting and easing me, that I have laid my hands upon him and have given him the blessing, so that – as they will recount – he is now filled with the spirit of wisdom. (Not my wisdom. Never mine. We have to be clear about that.) He will be the worthy successor, to lead my people into the Promised Land. For me it is nearly done, and my heart is uncertain. Not because I am forbidden to go into the Land (no mirage – he is wrong) but because of my great fault.

Joshua, I tell him, urgent to have it said, I have trespassed against the Lord. In my arrogance, I took his glory upon me as my own. I failed him in the wilderness – there, at the waters of Meribah. And now I am punished.

Yet Joshua is still smiling, his dark, compassionate face attentive to me. Did not the Lord, he reminds me, promise that you would see the Land stretched out before you, even though you might not enter it? And is not this more than was granted even to your brother, the Anointed Priest, dying upon an earlier mountain?

Yes, I acknowledge, straining to look around, aware of the now silent companies withdrawn from about me, respectfully distant. And so, I ruminate, out of all the old ones, and because of the Lord's enigmatic inflexibility, there are but the two of them left to lead my people forward: Joshua and Caleb. The new generations are fresh and young, free of all the resentments, the fretful carpings and rebellions. Ready to march into their Land, and to inherit it. And though the Lord has rightly punished me, he is now showing his mercy.

'Because of Meribah,' he had said long ago, 'thou shalt not go thither into the Land which I give the children of Israel.' Nevertheless, offering balm to ease my hurt, 'I shall cause thee to see it with thine eyes.' And so it is, and is it not enough? Have I not proclaimed his Name?

I can feel my dry lips moving stiffly, even as Joshua and his host grow dim. 'My teaching . . .' I raise my voice, obstinately, so as to reach my people. Have I not always reached them? Am I not in their bones? '. . . shall drop as the rain, my speech shall distil as dew, as the small rain upon tender grass, and as the showers upon the herb.'

Ah, well! I was always endangered by this kind of vanity, the aggression of the meek, and I know whence it springs.

Yet I, so easily swayed by pity and arrogance and wrath and uncertainty, so disastrously open to both the giving and receiving of contempt, I, in my absurd, opinionated way, have loved the Lord. And, also, I have loved my fractious and disobedient people.

I

The Cloven Tongue

A warm darkness, with the taint of fear. The lapping of water, the stickiness of pitch, the scratch of reeds. Then, brightness – a burst of gold and the heady gift of power.

These memories remain with me from earliest days. The darkness was in Egypt – my mother, Jochebed, concealing me when Pharaoh, jealous of our people's increase and fearing rebellion, ordered the new-born Hebrew boys to be thrown into the river. I lay in the deep recesses of the house, swaddled in darkness, comforted only by my mother's breast. Yet even with her milk I drank in the fear. It curdled in my stomach and reached out spiteful fingers to squeeze my unshaped mind. I fretted constantly, in unison with my mother's trembling.

Then came change. Always, the women were resourceful, not least Jochebed. I could smell new smells – the wet rushes of my basket and the pitch that oozed disgustingly over my garments, so that I beat my fists into the mess and howled with outrage. Then, lulled by the soft, lapping water, I slept, half-conscious of the scrape, scrape of the tall reed-bed into which I was more or less securely wedged.

Not a bright future, I should have appraised it, had I been of an age to voice my opinions. But Jochebed was cleverer than I, for next there was a splashing and a tugging, giggles of panting laughter, and I was turned nearly upside-down. When they opened the lid, fumbling at the skewer that closed it and giving little shrieks of excitement, there came a hot blast of sunlight, which struck across my unaccustomed eyes so that I screamed with scarlet fury. They moved back hastily, the giggly girls, flipping their pretty, wet hands and making small grimaces of disgust.

But then a new face hung over me, a face of authority which I recognised, even in the midst of my temper, as being set apart. Yet how much could I have apprehended, there on the river-bank, as my future swung in the balance? Nothing, of course, but I must have had the sense to clutch at the extended finger with my oily fist and then – how wise of me! – to cease my sobbing and regard her with an ecstatic smile.

And so the power and the glory began: the adopted darling, the young prince brought up under royal patronage.

Looking back, I can see that there was a string of improbabilities. Had it not been for Jochebed's ingenuity, successfully evoking the royal compassion; had it not been for the astute placing of my sister Miriam (Ah! That sister! That thorn of practicality in my flesh!) where she could so obligingly trip forward to recommend a certain wet-nurse; had it not been for my mother's inclusion within the royal household – why, I should surely have drowned in that river along with all my unfortunate small kinsmen.

As it was, I grew a cloven tongue along with my cloven mind.

Two mothers: my soft, warm, determined Jochebed and my indulgent, equally determined princess. Two ways of living: the heritage, carefully unfolded, of my Hebrew ancestry, set against the authority of an Egyptian prince. Two ambitions: to succour my people in the bleak misery of serfdom, yet gracefully to fill my idle, autocratic role of pampered son. There can be little doubt whence stems my lifelong hazard of self-satisfaction, my arrogance, my quick rages – as, equally, my awareness of dispossession, the timidity that passed for meekness, the indecision.

So I grew up, my father but a shadow on the fringe of my life, my mother and Miriam receding daily as I grew from sucking to a more princely fare, surrendered wholly, now, to my second mother. It was during this time, before I became fully aware of the havoc within me and the irreconcilable choices to be made, that my tongue began to betray me. Often it would stick clumsily against my teeth, defying my need to utter. Like my heart, like my head, it refused to go quietly in one direction, filling my mouth as two separate entities and struggling against itself. I would stand with hanging head, no longer the self-assured princeling but only a gangly youth, hot with confusion and a divided mind. Then, from the watchful ones, there would be scorn and impatience, a remembrance of my origins, the curl of a lip, and my world would dissolve about me. I never quite recovered a clarity of tongue. Always it was liable to expose my uncertainties.

Yet perhaps I did cradle within myself something of Jochebed's inventive tenacity, filtered down into her children: tempering my elder brother Aaron's lofty indifference, exacerbating Miriam's hard-mouthed assertiveness, and surfacing, at last, in my own stubborn, ultimately intractable obstinacy.

For I sought out my people. And when I did so, there occurred the first intimation of that twitching of the curtain which was to afflict me throughout my life.

I had crept out secretly to watch the gangs of Hebrew workmen, bending in long lines to build an Egyptian treasure-house, hauling at the brick-loads in the noonday heat so that when one man fell, another was forced into his place.

Perhaps it may have been the sun beating on my unprotected head, but as I stood there, discreetly observant, the workmen pulling on their ropes began to shimmer and evaporate. I was under a different sky, patched with cloud, in a dark, stained compound fenced by wire, with a huddle of squat brick buildings incongruous with the elegance of Egypt. Out of one of those buildings reared a chimney, from which there ascended long fumes of oily smoke. There were men standing around with whips, just as the Egyptian overseers would stand. Were standing. Yet these men were alien. Dogs with bright, sagacious eyes were straining at their leashes, each caught on a tight rein by its handler. And straggling across the yard there shuffled a long line of men and boys, some young, others grey-bearded, all naked and shivering. I gazed with horrified foreboding as the stark fresco of their bodies imprinted itself upon the heaving lines of our bricklayers sweating beneath the Egyptian sun. The guards did nothing, expressionless save for that identical contemptuous vacancy I had noted on the faces of the overseers.

Yet, and this was where my throat thickened and a bloody tide swept across my eyes, as they reached the doors to the abomination that awaited them, the scarecrow creatures straightened, thrust back bony shoulders and clasped the small boys who pressed against them, so that the children, too, threw up their heads and the whole pitiful crew broke into a song of passionate gratitude: 'Blessed be the Lord, the God of Israel. . . .'

Then, marching in a buoyant rhythm, no longer desolate but now as victors and untouchable, they sang their way into a Sheol that could never contain them, the doors closing on the rise and fall of their thin, exultant voices: 'Hear, O Israel: the Lord our God is one Lord.'

It was over. I stood once more in Egypt's sun, retching, while the sweat of agony poured down my body. Stumbling behind a pillar, I looked this way and that and, seeing an Egyptian smite one of my people, I killed him.

II

Neither Prince nor Judge

I tried, in haste, to bury the overseer in the hot, unyielding sand, still trembling and stupidly inadequate. But my act had been noted, and the story spread, so that those who waited now took their chance. Even the princess could not restrain the Pharaoh's eager wrath, and so, without farewells, I fled, for the second time in my life deprived of sonship.

But before I went, and before the story had been spread around, one of my own people spoke bitterly against me when I chose intemperately to interfere in a quarrel he had picked with another man.

'Who made thee a prince and a judge over us?' he cried with furious scorn, and I saw myself, suddenly, through the eyes of his contempt – neither fish nor flesh, but a mere empty shell of a boy, trying to ape the ways of the oppressors.

Who made thee prince? I quailed at my people's derision, knowing the answer. Who made thee judge? Indeed, untried and bumptious as I was, this was all too clear to me, even in my confusion. The taunt had been well earned. And even if the Pharaoh's death-edict had not followed so closely on the rumours, I should certainly have fled: anything to escape the humiliation of their disdain.

And so, for the first time, I found myself in the desert, as alone there and as sealed off from my known world as I had been in that early, skewered basket; drifting, now, ever eastward and south into the spare grazing lands of the people of Midian, and pondering as I went the words spoken to me in such anger.

It was an exacting life, on meagre rations and with no soft

couches, yet one which built up my languid muscles, stripped away the accumulated fat and sharpened my sight as I gazed into the long, vast, yellow distances. I became spare and agile and exceedingly tough. Yet my mind remained in a ferment of indecision. A prince? No longer; that I had forfeited, if ever I had merited such a title. A judge? I would stare at my face in desert pools and laugh at its dark-bearded reflection. Hardly the wise elder who might claim such a distinction. Did I desire to be a prince? Did I want to be a judge? I shuddered at such ideas in fits of bitter rejection, churning them over in my mind as I wandered aimlessly along the routes of the heavily laden spice caravans, or lingered a few weeks by an oasis to help with the flocks of a nomad tribe.

It was an inhospitable landscape, grey and yellow, brown and copper, purple and red: all sharp, hard edges that hurt the eyes like knives, the jagged mountains guarding ever deeper recesses of stony wasteland. It began to seem a living entity, waiting its time, ready to swallow this foolhardy intruder at his first mistake, eager for the smallest slip. Yet 'eager' is the wrong word, for it held no malice – only a barren, majestic indifference, an aloofness mirrored (or so it often seemed) in the insolent faces of the camels that trod its hidden ways. After all, it had been waiting a long time, and this untrammelled stranger was scarcely a tasty morsel. More to its liking must have been the signs of larger disasters: the heaped bones, the half-buried caravans seen, now and then, sticking out of the sand.

You had to earn the desert. That, I recognised. Many of those to whom I talked, laden with merchandise and making their way with all speed to the comforts of Egypt, would cast haunted glances behind them, glad to be almost safe, and fearful lest, in the last few weeks, the desert might pounce. Yet as I went ever deeper, forsaking the trade routes, I found a healing within its enormous solitudes. My body responded to the alternation of the broiling sun by day and the intense cold of the jewel-pricked sky by night. I would listen to the pulsing quiet, where all sounds became but individual silences within the great stillness of the desert: the soft silence of wind over sand, the skittering silence of tiny, hidden creatures, the grating silence of the ragged, cud-chewing, wild and fierce-horned goats and sheep. All the tiny noises, even the rare splashing of water over pebbles and the crackle of a nomad's fire, became caught up, for me, into that one vast, enduring soundlessness which surrounded me, always with an immense question mark. Neither prince nor judge. Then who?

I must have discovered something of myself and my needs – indeed, of my lack of needs – when I came at last to the tents of the priest Jethro. He lavished a fatherly care upon me and treated me as the son-in-law I eventually became, earning this reward because I had been of service to his daughters. It had happened at a desert well, when they were being threatened by wild mountain shepherds as they struggled to water Jethro's flocks. By that time I was a match for any shepherd and, besides, the daughters were attractive and it pleased me to show off my strength and my old manner of authority.

In the end, I was given Zipporah to wife, and when our first son was born I called him Gershom. I remember Zipporah's fiercely troubled eyes, dark with reproach at a name signifying 'stranger' and denoting my sense of exile.

But I am a stranger, I told her brutally, knowing it to be true, and caring only for the truth and nothing for the way she winced and caught her child resentfully to her.

Yet the child is no stranger, she rounded on me, tears of weakness and anger staining her cheeks, nor should you brand him as such. He belongs here, in the tents of Midian.

And I do not. It lay between us, deeper than any physical barrier, the knowledge that I might never be bound; I, a stranger to the hearths of men, and, from having sought them eagerly, as with Jethro and Zipporah, turning away and needing them no more. It was to plague me all my days: that passionate desire for a place of belonging, for the closely woven few who were flesh of my flesh and bone of my bone, while, in the very achievement of such felicity, I knew an immediate panic of rejection. For me, the huge, unwieldy throng of my unlicked people were all the family I would ever get. Or ever want.

I recall Zipporah as fiercely independent and naïvely superstitious. There was a time, on the journey back to Egypt, when I lay sick (but was it sickness or just the instinctive fear of return, even with the Pharaoh long since dead?). Then I watched helplessly as Zipporah briskly, and expertly, set about circumcising our second son with a sharp flint – all because she was credulously certain I should be punished with death were the rite not speedily performed.

Eventually she returned to her father and I was glad of it. All so determined, these women who constantly attempted to arrange my life. But was there not something in me, some weakness, which evoked their possessiveness? I knew only one, the Ethiopian woman, who wore a small, soft place in my heart. She came much later and brought with her, for the short time till Miriam destroyed it, a gentle grace, contentment, and the mercy of acceptance. It was not for very long. Yet she lingers where the others have been forgotten.

After the birth of Gershom, I wearied of the tents, the cackle of voices, the endless domesticity, wearied even of Jethro's quiet, searching wisdom. More and more I went out with the flocks, preferring the company of those tough, touchy, half-wild creatures to the bickering of Zipporah's sisters. I needed the wilderness to remove myself from the trodden oases and to search out hidden pastures, far off from other men's usage and discovered only with infinite toil and patience deep in some cleft of the hills.

Once free of my family, I was regenerate. For days, for weeks, I pushed restlessly south, crossing the unprofitable wasteland, scratching up food as best I could, wary of other herdsmen and concerned, always, to find fresh watering for my flock. I would stand while they grazed, staring at some bony range of distant hills. What is it you want of me? I would ask, my lips cracked and peeling. What have I to do with you? What are you trying to tell me? What is my task? And then, with increasing frequency: I cannot measure up. I am not able. I am afraid.

Occasionally, in the blinding sun, as I peered out from the shadow of a rock, I would catch a flicker of movement, sudden, and then as suddenly quenched. Movement where no movement could be. An overlapping of realities. Yet, thankfully, I received no visions of the future, still flinching from the sickness of what I had seen in Egypt. It was as if, in this vast, impervious place, I had lost the nerve-edges of receptivity; had passed out of communication with whatever it was that had burst in upon me; had now become, in some small measure, refined and small-ground and purified, so that my torn, unstable mind settled into itself, knitted together by the bleak integrity of this yellow wilderness.

Even so, I would catch those sudden flickers of light, as if patches of the desert were thrusting into flame. But when I looked again, they extinguished themselves and I decided it was a fault in my vision. I could feel the desert exerting its discipline and I watched it lovingly, surrendering my heart to its testing, rejoicing in its burnt-red rocks, its violet-shadowed distances. At night I would sit beside my fire, aware of black, velvet shapes as the mountains rose to meet the sky, conscious of the shaggy, ferocious dogs – my unsleeping guardians – who prowled the edges of the flock, conscious above all else of the silence beating softly into me. Listen, it said. Keep watch. And I would bury my head in my hands, not in despair but rather in a rapt adoration, and call upon the God of Abraham to show me my way.

III

The Burning Bush

I had searched so long (never worthy, or how in the end should I have hesitated?), pondering whether the Lord might open up a way for me to follow. Yet when the time came, I was not ready, and would have turned aside.

It so happened – though what is chance and what is a leading? – that I had eased my flock far down into the wasteland, to confront at last the mountain they call Horeb. Just another mountain, I thought, being parched and dusty and tired of wandering. No mark of impending promise and certainly no indication of the Lord's presence. How should there be?

There it was, part of the great mountain barrier that blocked my way. Clearly I had reached the end. The mountain told me so in unmistakable fashion, the rocky, golden walls rising in cumbrous prohibition. Now there was nothing left to do but to return, watering my flock in the newly discovered pastures until I arrived once more at the tents of Jethro.

I looked around me, the caked lines of weariness etched deep into my face and bearing an added passion of bitterness. I was at the back of the wilderness and still there was no answer to my gropings.

The day was quiet. All my days were quiet. Not even the clatter of a pebble disturbed the solitude of this place. Leading away into the flanks of the mountain, I could see deep shadows, blue-black against the yellow rock, the sigh of shaded pasture, a respite from the blistering sun which danced in the white-hot sky over the heads of my beasts. It was while I was on my way there, driving the flock and the now-eager dogs deeper into the cool protection of this rock fortress, that I saw the bush. Something about it caught my attention, one of those odd flickers of light, and when I looked again it seemed, to my dazzled sight, to be on fire and burning with a clear, soundless brilliance.

I shaded my eyes, while the dogs drove the sheep expertly towards their grazing and the distant trickle of a stream. Was it the sun, distorting my vision? Or was there indeed a scrubby bush, burning fiercely and yet, as I noted with a frown of disbelief, in no way being consumed.

For a long time I stood there, hungry, and with a part of my mind occupied by the sharp yelpings of the dogs. Only a mirage. I shrugged and turned away, longing for the sudden plunge into shade. Once against the shelter of the rock wall, with the welcome chill of unwarmed stone cutting blessedly into my bones, I looked back yet again.

I could see it more distinctly now. The bush was completely afire, the flames fanning out on either side and roaring as a tall fountain into the quivering air. It shone with a reddish glow, a deep rose colour like the petals of a flower, catching my heart with its sudden beauty. This was no natural burning, sun-induced, and I felt my throat constrict and my knees turn to water. Let me not see it, I shouted wordlessly. Let it put itself out. I want nothing from it. I have my sheep.

And so I turned away, calling to the dogs, settling my flock and attending then to my own needs. Later I rested, but uneasily, propped against a boulder and shutting my mind to the implacable silence of the place. Presently I got up, uncertain but defiant, to look furtively into the noonday heat. The bush was still burning, and ever more fiercely, the rose-red flames now holding glints of blue and orange and a greenish fire. The structure of twisted stock and branches and small, tough leaves was easily visible within the burning. Not a shoot disturbed, not a twig destroyed.

Perhaps, I thought, kicking at a stone, I should go and examine this marvel. But now I was sweating with fear because I knew that it was intended for me. And that I might refuse it. And that acceptance, were I to offer it, would be intolerable.

So I hesitated, knowing full well that after fighting with myself I should turn aside from that cool place within the mountain cleft and go out to discover why the bush did not blacken and die.

It was farther away than I had thought, and I called to one of the dogs, posting him at the entrance to the mountain pasture, just where the small stream spent itself in the dust. A safeguard against my return. I remembered the many tales of travellers in the desert rashly straying but a few yards from their caravan, only to lose all sense of direction.

But it was not just the fire which troubled me (undoubtedly, said my common sense, due to some freak illusion of the violent sun). For as I reluctantly approached, I could see not only the bush, untouched, but a shape within the flames which, I decided, could not possibly be there. It was, or so it seemed to be, a towering thing, enveloped in the fire yet independent of it; a thing with soaring wings (or were they, after all, but flames?) and a countenance that blinded me. Even while I was busy rejecting it, I knew it for what it was. Yet still I refused to see it, lowering my eyes and shaking with apprehension. And still the thing confronted me, with majesty and power, standing with its feet planted easily upon the flames and its great hands raised up in blessing.

A malakh, I whispered to myself, stumbling almost to my knees, a messenger. The angel of the Lord God, summoning me to this strange trysting-place. I licked dry lips, remembering what it was: one who moves before the face of the Lord to clear his path and to announce his coming. And, as the great figure, brilliant with fire, drew me, still unwilling, across the stony strip of desert, I had at last to admit its presence. Kneeling now in the sandy soil, I crouched awkwardly before the bush, while the malakh blazed steadily in showers of gold and, from behind its vast and silent form, a Voice called upon my name. 'Moses,' It cried, and again, 'Moses.'

What must I do? I went on kneeling there, my legs pressed into the sharp-edged stones, and I laid my head upon the ground and heard my own voice coming as if from a long distance, offering myself up to That which waited beyond the malakh: 'Here am I.'

Afterwards the words spoken between us were locked away in my mind, a treasure to be taken out and examined from time to time, that I might learn the full meaning of the responsibility laid upon me.

For the Lord had remembered his covenant with our ancestors, and had listened with pity to those who laboured now in bondage.

'I know their sorrows.'

This he said to me, out of the flame of fire. And as the bush burned, the Voice which reached me came from within the heart of it – I, prostrated in the holy place and hiding my face from the glory. He spoke to me of an unbelievable land, flowing, he told me, with milk and honey, where his people were to find peace after they had been led out of Egypt. And then, at last, he besought me tenderly, saying: 'Come now therefore . . . ' – and I flinched with terror – 'and I shall send thee unto Pharaoh, that thou mayest bring forth my people. . . .'

I cringed before him, not because of the immensity of the task but because I remembered how rightfully my people had repudiated me and because I saw myself to be inadequate – a mere herdsman, roughened by desert ways, and with a tongue ever liable to betray me.

So I wept, aware of my deficiencies and said to the Lord: 'Who am I, that I should go unto Pharaoh?' adding, defensively and perhaps somewhat tartly, that I was unfitted to bring anybody out of Egypt or anywhere else.

Was it my fancy, or did the flames leap up more fiercely? Yet there was no heat, nor did they shrivel me, and the Lord refrained from chiding. Instead, he told me, with great patience, that he would be with me through all the hazards. (But was that to be enough?) Also – and this I could not understand – that when I had brought his people out of bondage (but not before – not *before*?), they would be shown a token of my leadership on this very mountain of Horeb where I would be seen to serve him.

For a moment, I raised my head, gazing into the fringes of the flames, through the haze of which the shape of the mountain appeared to dance. I nodded to myself, thinking of my sheep, watered now, and content with the mountain's cool pastureland. As with the sheep, then so with the people, and perhaps I might manage to be in some such relationship to the people as the wary sheepdog to the sheep.

Yet, remembering the contempt I had aroused, I was still afraid, feeling I knew rather better than the Lord the kind of proof they would require and without which they would receive me in the same derision as they had sent me forth.

'When I come to the children of Israel,' I said from a tightening throat, 'and shall say unto them, the God of your fathers hath sent me unto you . . .' – I could feel my tongue grow thick – 'and they shall say to me, What is his name?. . .' Again, that accursed reluctance, my conviction of imperfection, knotting up the strings of my voice so that in the end I blurted out in sweating desperation, 'What shall I say unto them?' repeating frantically in my heart, O Lord my God, *what shall I say unto them*?

And the answer came: 'I AM THAT I AM.'

These words, or so it seemed, issued from the rose of fire, not sternly, not thundering, but gentle as a touch and powerful as the rocks. For one strange, disappearing moment what was then spoken became for me the single point that encompasses all meaning, the song lying at the back of silence, the music of stars, the voice of mountains and the message that the desert had been delivering to me in the long weeks of journeying, the answer to all that I had desired to know.

'Thou shalt say,' came the Lord's bidding, 'I AM hath sent me to you.'

Again, that blinding moment, the whole of my search made known, the Lord's voice revealing the inmost secret, reaching me out of the desert's solitude.

The moment passed, quivering into silence like the dying note of a struck bell. And, to my timid mind, the answer I had received, though I wrote it into my being, seemed not such as would impress my authority upon the people. Ah, yes! Here we have it! That quaking need to establish my self!

Indeed, the Lord persevered with me, explaining how I might the more easily approach the King of Egypt by pretending only a three-day journey to prepare our religious rites, and promising to afflict Egypt when we were refused this small privilege. I was not listening, obsessed by my certainty of rejection.

'But', I pointed out, tenaciously, 'they will not believe me. . . . They will say, the Lord hath not appeared unto thee.'

It was then that the Lord, exasperated, told me to cast my shepherd's staff upon the ground and, when I did so, it became a snake from which I grovelled away in panic. But when, under the Lord's compulsion, I stretched out my hand and took it by its tail, it became once more my stalwart rod. By such devices, and with even the ability to turn water into blood, the Lord sought to convince me that I, in turn, might convince my people. Still I was obdurate, revealing to him my greatest fear.

'O Lord,' I confessed, 'I am not eloquent, neither heretofore nor since thou hast spoken unto thy servant. For I am slow of speech, and of a slow tongue.'

This was my shame, and I covered my eyes and knew that the tears crept through my fingers. There was a silence. Had I touched his heart? Or could it be that the Lord himself was perplexed? – as perhaps he might well be.

Then he said, as if with a sigh: 'Who hath made man's mouth? Or who maketh a man dumb, or deaf, or seeing, or blind? Is it not I the Lord? Now, therefore, go and I shall be with thy mouth and teach thee what thou shalt speak.'

Perhaps it may appear to be beyond belief, yet I continued unconvinced, having after all known myself and my disabilities all my life, and thinking that probably the Lord might not have had time to notice them. It was then, indeed, that he became angry, kindled as the fire out of which he spoke. There was contempt . . .

'Is there not Aaron thy brother the Levite? I know that he can speak well. . . .'

Here indeed was humiliation. I felt the Lord turn from me. My own stupidity, my lack of faith. In that moment, when I refused to rise above myself, I lost part of my mission. Yet it was with relief, oh yes, with the knowledge of a burden removed, that I heard the Lord name Aaron as my spokesman. And such was my joy that I hardly realised how greatly he was continuing to trust me, in spite of my defection. For the words which Aaron was to speak were to come, it seemed, not directly from the Lord but mediated through myself.

'Thou shalt speak unto him, and put the words in his mouth, and I shall be with thy mouth.'

And then the comfort! Ah, the comfort! The caressing, dangerous, testing words of power.

'He shall be to thee a mouth, and thou shalt be to him as God.'

But I did not see the danger – only, in that moment, as the flames began to fade, the promise.

─── IV ───

Let My People Go

The glory had departed, and I found myself empty.

I lay face down upon the stones, sensing the withdrawal of power, aware of desolation. No fire, no messenger, no Voice. I was alone. I lay there for a long time in a kind of death.

At length, raising my head, I saw that I had crawled into the shelter of the bush. Like me, it was bereft of ecstasy. Dingy now, and extinguished, it remained precisely as it had always been, dry and tough and tenacious, built to withstand the deprivations of the desert.

Shaking myself free of anguish, I regarded it soberly. Built to withstand deprivation. Was it possible? Could I, perhaps, become that bush? Take on its toughness and tenacity? Even, if need be, its dryness – although that, indeed, would be a lonely thing to do. Had not the wilderness already shaped me, as the bush itself had been shaped? Was I not, like the bush, now a little more able to endure? Even able, as the bush so clearly was, to become truly myself? After all, that ordinary piece of scrub had housed the fire, had contained the messenger, had been – yes – the mouthpiece of the Lord. And still it retained the structure of its own essential being.

I sat up, gazing confusedly at the surrounding waste. Could I, an ordinary being, house the fire of God? Show myself as his messenger? Become his mouthpiece? I gathered courage, aware of difference within myself, of a strange new yeast at work upon the shifting grain of my being.

I got to my feet, bent down to retrieve my staff. Then, hesitating, I turned and bowed myself low, with humility and a queer spurt of gratitude, towards the bush. Its small leaves scratched and rattled in a rising puff of wind.

I withdrew backwards from the place.

When I reached the dog, I let my hand touch briefly his head, on that flat, sensitive part between the ears where animals bear the worries of their world. After we had returned to the flock, I sank down and slept until nightfall.

Perhaps, after all, the Lord repented of his choice, for certainly the journey with Zipporah and the children, when we had left Jethro to return to Egypt, was a disastrous one. In spite of the Lord's assurance that all the men were now dead who had sought to kill me, I did not believe him, and so fell ill. With fear, as I have said.

It was a time when all my senses were blurred and I was caught as into a dream, unable to disentangle it from reality. I knew that I could hear the Lord's voice admonishing me to continue my journey. I was, he said, to tell Pharaoh that the people of Israel were to him as his first-born son. I was to say that the Lord's first-born must therefore be released to come and serve the Lord. I was to say – and here my eyes and my ears were stopped with terror – that if the Lord's first-born were hindered in any way from this purpose, then he, the Lord, would kill all the first-born of the children of Egypt.

I heard the Lord's instruction but I could not move and my tongue, as of old, was thick with foreboding. I lay in my fever, and watched helplessly as he advanced – or so it seemed – upon me, his hands raised. Against me? Or was it in blessing? I could not tell. Only that Zipporah was there, standing between us like a tigress and flinging our son's freshly severed foreskin at the Lord's feet. I could hear her screaming, as if a long way off.

'Surely', she raved, careless of the Lord's anger, her shadow looming over the tent, 'a bridegroom of blood art thou to me.'

I could not stop her, and again she screeched defiance.

'A bridegroom of blood art thou, because of the circumcision.'

So the Lord let me alone. Perhaps he saw her as a she-animal in defence of its mate. Perhaps he thought to acknowledge her courage. Pehaps he decided she had argued logically. Afterwards, I could not clearly recall what had happened, and Zipporah herself became sullen and intractable, with a thin mouth, refusing to comment.

Only: He would have killed you, she hurled at me, though not in a voice as if it would have mattered to her. Well, she returned to Jethro. . . .

After this, it seemed as if things might work out better. I went out to meet my brother Aaron and, though he was nine years older, he listened to me with awe and served me as if he were the younger. I remembered that the Lord had said it would be so: that I would be to Aaron as God. But I shied away from such a thought, quelling my sudden elation. Perhaps, I told myself soberly, there may have been something left of that desert experience, enough anyway to cause Aaron to give me his solemn attention. Well, he was a solemn man. Taller than I, and with more dignity.

So at first, when we met the elders of my people, they too listened, and the people rejoiced. In our great foolishness we went to Pharaoh with light hearts, thinking it would be only a matter of days before we could start on our journey. We explained, as if it were a simple thing, that the God of the Hebrews had met with us, bidding us make a three-day journey into the desert, where we must offer sacrifice (longer than three days we considered imprudent). We added, innocently, that if we did not obey him, he – our God – might become angry and afflict us with disease. Both of us imagined that in this we had been cunning, particularly in stressing the probable, if not inevitable, infectious spread of such sickness. Indeed, it seemed obvious that Pharaoh, in his alarm, would the more willingly let us go. We even dared to coerce him a little. Looking back, I can see how ill-advisedly we must have appeared to pit our unknown God against the whole might of Egypt. We told him that our departure was required of Pharaoh by the Lord God of Israel. And here we chanted the demand which would have sounded so impudent: 'Let my people go.'

This was our mistake, for he turned on us in fury. 'Who is the Lord,' he squealed, 'that I should hearken unto his voice to let Israel go? I know not the Lord.' And he settled himself back, coldly, staring at us with grim satisfaction. 'And, moreover, I shall not let Israel go.'

But of course we were essential to him. Why should he let us go? It was in that moment, though I believe Aaron was not quick enough to sense it, that I understood what lay before us. A chill

— 33 —

occupied my heart. Never, I saw, would we break free by way of threats or clever tricks, not even with blandishments, but only – only – when Pharaoh himself had need to be rid of us. What I did not realise was the time this would take, the wearying days merging into months, the months into years, while through it all Pharaoh heaped burden upon burden on our people.

Naturally, the people were quick to blame us (especially over the bricks, when they must find their own straw for the making), and Pharaoh equally quick to call them idle, this tale of sacrificing to the Lord being but an excuse to escape from honest labour.

'The Lord look upon you, and judge,' said my people fiercely to Aaron and me, adding that we had succeeded only in making them abhorrent in the eyes of Pharaoh, and that the tumult we had caused had put a useful sword into the hands of the Egyptians.

I admit it: I complained bitterly to the Lord, accusing him of mistreating his people – with, of course, the best of intentions – and asking, over and over again, why he had sent me into Egypt. I accused him, in my injured and ignorant pride, of going the wrong way about things, so that his people would never now find deliverance. But it was no use. The Lord invariably won these arguments, reminding me patiently (as if I were not out of my mind so to confront him!) that he was Jehovah, the God of Abraham and Isaac and Jacob; also that he was aware of his covenant and did indeed hear the groaning of his people. Again and again he renewed his promise to bring us out of bondage. But as time passed it seemed as if we would live and die under the whip of the oppressor.

Because of this, we resorted to demonstrating the Lord's superior power, seeking to prove to Pharaoh that our God was stronger than his priests. I remember these tricks with infinite distaste, conscious that Aaron enjoyed them to the full, since it was he who was thought to exert his own pre-eminence and call up the magic. For my part, I detested playing with rods that turned into snakes – a feat easily emulated by Pharaoh's magicians (though I have to admit that Aaron's snake deftly swallowed all those other illusions). But shape-shifting, I considered, was unworthy of the Lord God of Israel.

And when we came to the plagues, the turning of the river water into blood with its resulting filthy corruption, and the whole string of disasters – the frogs and the lice and the flies, not to mention the cattle dying of disease, the boils, the hailstones, the swarm of locusts and the pall of darkness – well, then I could see, though at first the magicians had matched us step by step, that they were eventually defeated and discredited. Even so, it gave me intense unease.

Both Aaron and Miriam rejoiced over our successes, and even Pharaoh began to appear a little frightened by our God, confessing, in the extremity of all the unpleasantnesses and sickness and other offensive occurrences, that he must somehow have sinned to have brought this punishment upon Egypt. We, of course, in our own settlement, remained unafflicted.

Yet as I watched these so-called successes (taking months to arrange and months to bring to a halt) and as I saw how they made no lasting mark upon the king of Egypt (since, after each frightened promise of our release, he at once repented of his repentance), I began to use my wits.

I looked around me, remembering the reddened waters, and the way the river stank and the fish died and the pollution was such that no man might drink. And I could not be sure that it had been blood, but rather thought it some kind of poison out of the soil in the river-bed, or brought down from the upper sources. I watched carefully when the plague of frogs crawled and hopped about the land, and I remembered I had heard tales of such infestations from the merchants who crossed the wilderness – similarly of the lice and flies breeding in the dirt left over from the tainted waters. I saw the cattle grow sick as they cropped the meagre grazing, and then the horrid boils suffered by the Egyptians when in desperation they tried to eat the diseased carcases. I saw, too, how the harvest was destroyed by hail, and how the clouds of locusts devoured what was left of it, and how the sky became obscured by that curious, heavy blanket of air which hung over the entire kingdom.

The desert had taught me much. I knew how swiftly a climate could change, how freak movements of air and sudden swarms of insects could damage the land; how men could be weakened with sores when their cattle had died sick. I saw our own survival as being due more to our abstemious living than to magic, and, noticing how each of these plagues would linger on, declining but slowly, I thought that much of what had happened would have happened anyway.

I came to the conclusion that only the deep superstitions of an uneducated people, whipped up by magical ritual at a time of unrest and fear, had made any other interpretation possible. But I kept my thoughts to myself, not even sharing them with Aaron. Specially not with Aaron. We had been upheld, and the plagues had worked to our advantage.

—— V ——

The Sending

We needed more than omens, and sometimes, as the months passed and Pharaoh piled ever more monstrous tasks upon my people, I found it difficult not to flinch when accused of being the cause of their distress. I had, they told me, deluded them with false hopes, and all I had achieved was to goad Pharaoh into a fury of revenge which had fallen on them rather than on me. There was truth in what they said, for both Aaron and I were exempt from Pharaoh's malevolence, eyed a little askance even by Pharaoh himself for what were considered to be our powers, so that one and all avoided upsetting us. We even became persons of recognised distinction, and I could tell that Pharaoh, always emotionally unhinged and therefore dangerous, began to feel a curiously ambivalent respect for us: an explosive mixture of fear and anger and curiosity, which we reciprocated. It developed into an odd relationship, one of hostile tolerance, a need within each for the exacerbation of the other.

It took some time for these ideas to drop into my mind and take root there, but then I began to glimpse the Lord's wisdom in delaying our departure from Egypt. Perhaps it was necessary that we should not have gone during those first untried moments of exultation. Perhaps we needed the discipline of that endless waiting, of testing ourselves against our doubts, of recovering from the spurious hopes and plunging fears that accompanied each unsuitable demonstration of the Lord's power. Perhaps we were supposed to temper ourselves a little and to accept patience as the needful preliminary to a journey that should not be lightly undertaken towards a heritage which must not fall too easily into our laps.

All this I thought about, certain that the Lord was leading us, but certain also that the inmost fashion of it was not for our entire knowing. He spoke many times with me in those days, I the interpreter of strange, exacting requirements, obedient even when I could not understand, and walking among my people with a listening look upon my face. At such times Aaron was afraid of me, and his eyes would fall before mine, while Miriam would frown petulantly yet know herself unable to speak in my presence. Only the boy Joshua, if I met him by the way, would go down on one knee, his face bearing something of the rapture that may have been upon my own.

In those conversations with the Lord, I moved – or so it seemed – within a closed bubble of light where none might touch me. I sensed new growth. In the desert it had been first my body and then my mind that had been tried. Here in Egypt it was the spirit, shaped into the necessary instrument. Increasingly, even though I longed to remain apart and shut away from action and decision, I began to recognise the need to integrate my two worlds: the silent, inner world where the Lord spoke in my mind, and the shrill, warm, taxing world of my headstrong people.

Indeed, before the tenth, decisive punishment came to afflict Egypt, I was drawn out of myself into something I was unwilling to admit. I have said how Aaron enjoyed all the evidences of power, how almost gleefully that otherwise dignified man would swallow those serpents into his own illusory rod. I think that, even then, he was beginning to breed within himself a jealousy towards me, rebellious that it was my tongue, my mouth, however inarticulate, through which the Lord spoke to him. He began to hold soft, tireless unburdenings with our sister Miriam, always withdrawn from me and casting anxious glances around. Seeing them so often together, and watching how Miriam dominated him, I learned that my lofty Aaron was insubstantial. And I knew from my own uncertainties that, in his weakness, he could become guileful and so damage me.

Me? No, that did not matter. But he must not be allowed to damage the Lord's purpose. I remembered my bush, an ordinary piece of scrub among its ordinary fellows. Aaron and I, too, were ordinary, compounded of ordinary emotions and subject to ordinary imperfections. And what had the desert said to me? Keep watch. So I kept watch, and decided that, as soon as it became appropriate, I should give Aaron some real power, that he might become somewhat satisfied, that he might, harmlessly, preen himself a little.

I was beginning to weigh up the unpredictable emotions with which I was surrounded. And always I remained apart, listening, but never participating in the endless chatter. This was my gift from the desert – disconcerting for those who felt they might use me. In those years, so filled for me with petty irritations, false hopes and resentment, I think I became myself. Aware of the dark places within me from which my weakness stemmed and where perhaps cruelty lurked, but, I believe, a more complete human being than I had been.

During this period, one of unrest and bitterness for my people, Aaron had no power to hurt me, and Miriam stood behind him, as it were his shadow. And if she urged on his mounting jealousy, feeding it with her own busybody air of importance, the two of them were meek and obedient in my presence. But I became more and more uneasy over Aaron's arrogance, and quailed when I caught Miriam's following gaze, malicious and greedy. They were clever enough, though, to understand that without me there was no future, and their small jibes (made, I suspected, more readily to my people than to me), even when they pricked me, did not lessen my substance as the mouthpiece of the Lord.

I noticed – how could I fail to? – that they were never rebuked by the Lord for their petty insolence. This puzzled me, yet perhaps the Lord knew I needed such a spur to keep me one step ahead, always alert and wary, husbanding my will and my single passion that Egypt should let my people go.

It was during this time that I was shown another glimpse into the future. It came during the great darkness, when Egypt was overshadowed and desolate. We had only just escaped the locusts, a bad time for Pharaoh, when he had sent for us, beating his breast as usual and telling us he had sinned against the Lord our God (always ready to placate that which might perhaps prove the more powerful) and beseeching us to take away this death. So I had gone out with Aaron and had entreated the Lord, for indeed the locusts were too much to bear. And if Aaron had not noticed that a sudden, fierce west wind was blowing up anyway, I had certainly detected it, so that while Aaron was busy upon his ritual, I listened with extended arms as the wind came roaring down upon us, taking away the locusts and leaving a clear sky.

This left a heaviness upon me, since I knew that I must participate in the magic and knew also that it would avail us nothing. In this I had reason, for Pharaoh recovered from his fright and, as before, refused to let us go. I felt burdened by the ebb and flow of his moods, and burdened when, in obedience, I once more stretched out my hands towards heaven, just as a thickening, foggy darkness descended over us like a pall of smoke.

This time Pharaoh was even more terrified, especially when I stood before him with my renewed demand and he could scarcely see me through the gloom. 'Go ye, serve the Lord,' he spat at me bitterly. At times he was like a vicious cat, and I knew his claws. 'Only let your flocks and your herds be stayed.'

I sighed, not moving my ground, and argued wearily, saying that our cattle must go with us, being necessary for the sacrifice and the subsequent feasting. But Pharaoh refused to agree, crouched in his chair and mouthing at me.

The wrangle dragged on, and in the end he shrieked at me with the voice of insanity: 'Get thee from me, take heed to thyself. See my face no more, for the day thou seest my face thou shalt die.'

I think I replied patiently, yet it was from a leaden spirit.

'Thou hast spoken well. I shall see thy face again no more.'

And so we parted.

After that, I went away by myself, unseen in the pitch black, and sat down in the open near the river-bank. There was just the faintest sound of dripping moisture around me, together with the swift rushing of the water. I was enclosed in oppressive sound and a sticky obscurity, and I stared blankly into nothing, my heart acknowledging defeat. The soft, wet darkness seeped into me. There was no place, no life, no substance. Only the river beat relentlessly into my head until it blotted out my senses, becoming now a river of time passing. Moments, days, years came pressing down upon me in my desolation; I suffocated in the storm of their passage. I gaped into the surrounding blackness, aware of the centuries falling and falling, of being crushed beneath millennia. And at last, when my breathing had stopped and I could bear no more, I saw a faint rift in the darkness, a clouded gleam through which I seemed to step, entering a quiet room – large, and shadowed, with a light burning steadily before a curtain.

Above the curtain, fixed against the wall, were two rounded tablets, seemingly of stone and inscribed with letters. For a moment, as my mind took over in a burst of amazed terror, the vision broke into fragments and I was left again in darkness. But I knew, with absolute clarity, that the tablets were mine. They belonged to me, for I had made them. Not in this place and not in this time, yet in the time to come which was before the time of that place. Then, I would make them and they would be in my hands. This I knew.

I made a great effort to annul my will, and the fragments swung back into a complete picture. There were men in strange garments with small caps upon their heads and pale scarves about their shoulders. Not in my time, I told myself, with a rush of exultation. Not in my place. Though certainly they were my people. Then I was aware of a voice, lifted up in a tongue that was strange and yet familiar, and the words struck into my heart with pain and fear and awe.

'And it shall come to pass, if ye shall hearken diligently unto my commandments which I command you this day, to love the Lord your God, and to serve him with all your heart and with all your soul, that I will give the rain of your land in its season. . . .'

A young man faced me across the room. He had a soft, thin face, and dark eyes that stared straight into my own. Only, he did not see me. His gaze was brooding, as if he might be looking back down centuries, yet we did not meet. A faint smile curved his lips. It could have been a smile of welcome, but the eyes held no sign of recognition.

'Take heed to yourselves, lest your heart be deceived, and ye turn aside, and serve other gods, and worship them; and the anger of the Lord be kindled against you, and he shut up the heavens, that there be no rain, and that the land yield not her fruit; and ye perish quickly from off the good land which the Lord giveth you. . . .'

The voice was old but firm, talking of my people's iniquity and the Lord's displeasure as if both remained always a likely reality, yet with a peace upon the words and the acceptance of imperishable truth.

'Therefore shall ye lay up these my words in your heart and in your soul; and ye shall bind them for a sign upon your hand, and they shall be for frontlets between your eyes. . . .'

But this I did not understand.

'. . . And ye shall teach them your children, talking of them when thou sittest in thine house, and when thou walkest by the way, and when thou liest down, and when thou risest up. . . .'

The voice was gentle, and the people swayed to and fro, their faces intent and their white scarves dipping like waterfalls.

'And thou shalt write them upon the door posts of thine house, and upon thy gates: that your days may be multiplied and the days of your children, upon the land which the Lord sware unto your fathers to give them, as the days of the heavens above the earth.'

The voice was triumphant. But as suddenly as it had come, this sending into the future began to fade. I could feel energy withdrawn from me, as into a vortex, and I found myself once more in the middle of the dark fog that was Egypt. I was standing with my arms raised and those distant words echoing inside me, so that my soul burned with a passionate ecstasy.

For they were my own words. Words I had not yet uttered but which, when the Lord's time was ready, I should, as his mouthpiece, teach my people.

I looked around, seeing only the blank pall of fog, hearing only the drip and wash of water. Yet there, in that incredibly distant future, in that unknown place, I knew that my as yet unspoken words were to be pondered and taught. My people (and here I wept, joining my tears to the moisture of my garments) – my people would still be upon the face of the earth to offer their praise to the Lord God of Israel.

I fell down upon the wet sand, as once I had fallen before the bush. I saw time stretching out before me, a thousand thousand years, and my people suffering and dying, yet always the remnant surviving and increasing and remaining as witnesses to the Lord's mercy.

So I lay there, quiescent, until at last I heard my name cried aloud, and then a foot stumbled over me, and it was the young boy, Joshua, come to find me.

VI

The First-born

The time between the plague of darkness and the plague of the first-born was the most bitter we had known. Pharaoh drove his overseers fanatically, giving them licence to maltreat us in every imaginable way. They, in turn, drove my people with a savagery they had never shown before, extracting from us an insensate pace of labour we had not believed lay within our power. Paradoxically, it was also a time when my people found most favour in the sight of Pharaoh's servants: driven so ferociously, yet uncontaminated by the plagues, we were indispensable, unflaggingly at work under sickly taskmasters.

Watching all this, I was afraid. How should any nation, suffering as Egypt had suffered, relinquish these labourers? At the same time I had never been so alive and filled with hope. Both the fear and the hope jangled within me. At this nethermost pit of our four centuries in Egypt, when we were faced with failure and had slight prospect of ever breaking free, it seemed to me that the Lord's hand was over us as never before, gathering up his beaten people and binding them into the faithful instrument of his will.

That it would be a time of terror, I did not doubt, for I remembered the words the Lord had spoken in my sickness: that I should go to Pharaoh and threaten him with the death of his first-born. These words, forgotten till now, were once again taking possession of my mind, the Lord relentlessly repeating them and slowly crushing me into action with the force of his demands. And deep in my bones – with much dread – I sensed that the time was now upon us when Pharaoh would lose the apple of his eye, and his people likewise.

For weeks I shut my ears, though I could not shut out the Lord's voice. Looking around me, I saw a devastated land, a people struggling to pull themselves out of disease. What was more likely, in the natural course of events, that many were still to die? Especially those first-born who were but partly grown to manhood, working now beyond their strength, in particular the still-cradled first-born, since indeed they were fragile.

In those days I envied Aaron his uncompromising and somewhat insensitive assurance. He believed with passionate sincerity that the punishments befalling the Egyptians had come about not as natural happenings producing a logical result but solely through the power of our ritual. Not, of course, through our own power. I would not discredit Aaron, nor would he have been so presumptuous. But he saw the ritual as an independent channel for the Lord's arbitrary anger, he and I being the vessels of that wrath, and effectively calling down power where no power would otherwise be.

I think he sensed my doubts or, rather, my feeling that the Lord's methods were more subtle than we knew, and that Aaron's way of looking at them was dangerously akin to a pagan tribesman invoking capricious, coercive magic. Even though I was aware – who more so? – of the Lord's continual guidance, I found it difficult to persuade myself that he would stoop to a usurpation, indeed a violation, of the natural order of the earth. This I could not fully convey to Aaron but, in some region of my being, clogged under my disobedient tongue, I was certain that the power we were using was one that flowed along with the harmony of life – not a manipulation or a conjuring, but a harnessing. The result may have been inevitable with or without the harnessing, but men believe what they wish to believe, which is not necessarily what they see.

Even more curiously, I knew that the Lord, in his anger, was also grieving. But this also I could not express to Aaron. Indeed, when he saw my face as the first-born began to die, he laughed at me. Fierce laughter, with no amusement in it. Do you not remember, his voice rasped coldly, your basket in the reeds? When the Egyptians had killed off all our new-born babes? And is not this day in some fashion a retribution, a levelling of the score?

I saw his logic, but could only shake my head. I remember that I muttered something – my tongue immediately crippled – about the need to love our neighbour as ourself, aware that this was something the Lord would teach us. Later. But Aaron merely shrugged and turned away. It was easy to irritate him at that time, and I knew full well the burden he carried.

When the first of the first-born died, it was the child of Pharaoh. I had not thought ever to face him again, but in the night, as the boy was taken and as there came to his ears the crying of his people when their own children began to die, he sent for us. He seemed in that moment but an old grey monkey of a man, unable to look us in the eyes, his shaking hand across his mouth, his voice now strangely quiet. 'Rise up,' he croaked through his fingers, 'get you forth from among my people, both ye and the children of Israel. And go, serve the Lord, as ye have said.'

There lay a great silence between us in which we heard the women wailing.

'Take both your flocks and your herds,' he went on, still in that same dead voice, 'as ye have said, and be gone.'

We turned and left him then – Aaron tall in his jubilant dignity, knowing that this time the words would hold, I shaking with compassion in the face of Pharaoh's mortal sorrow.

After this, and amid the rising misery of the Egyptians, we packed our possessions and gathered together our cattle and our flocks. I had already instructed my people what they must do: each family should take a lamb without blemish and kill it, then sprinkle its blood upon their doorposts. This, I told them, was so that the Lord should see the mark and pass over their dwellings in peace, and death should not enter as it had done in the houses of the Egyptians.

I understood full well that the Lord was able to recognise his own without this sign of blood, but it seemed to me that my people, already humming like a taut wire against the surrounding lament, might fear for their lives and break in panic unless they had the comfort of this small piece of magic. Was it not warranted? Surely?

Moreover, I turned the occasion into a perpetual observance which my people were ever to re-enact in praise of the Lord for bringing them out of Egypt.

The meal itself was undertaken hurriedly, our people wary and sheltering in their homes: the lamb roasted, the bread unleavened because of our urgency, the herbs bitter with our present remembrance of what had now so suddenly become our past. We ate in haste, readied ourselves in haste, and departed in haste, perhaps a little frightened at how the Egyptians came thronging round us, pressing gold and silver and jewels into our hands – anything to speed us on. We observed, with growing relief, their passionate anxiety to see the back of us. For unless you go, they told us, 'we are all dead men'.

And so we left Rameses, the city our forced labour had helped to build, taking with us the bones of our ancestor Joseph, and travelling by night – that great, silent, timeless night of the Lord.

I have a memory of Pharaoh, his head now raised to watch us go. I think it was I alone who heard his quiet petition: '. . . and bless me also'.

So I remembered him, his power over us now broken, and in my heart I blessed him. For who was I to withhold such consolation from however vicious and degenerate a man? We met, at some deeper level than our human frailty, and for a moment we touched. And out of my compassion – and my own need – I found, between us, a reconciling.

VII

The Cloud and the Fire

We came out of Egypt armed and in reasonable order. Yet I could see how vulnerable we were, not only to attack by hostile tribes but to those more insidious enemies of doubt and despair. Before us, had we known, lay the interminable years of wandering. But that knowledge we were spared.

The direct way into Canaan was but a week's journey, a straight highway and much travelled: in time of peace, by traders; in time of war, by armies. This was naturally the way our people were set on going, and it was only after fierce argument that Aaron and I were able to turn them. Many times during the next forty years I regretted that decision. Yet the Lord had cautioned me not to confront the warring Philistines with my flock, as yet undisciplined. For my part, I was glad to obey, drawn as ever to the wilderness, and believing it safer for us to lose ourselves in a great loop around the Sea of Reeds. Here, shut within an unknown, desolate land, Pharaoh, should he pursue us, might well count us disastrously entangled – to wander unprotected and, eventually, to die.

Indeed, had Pharaoh so envisaged our fate, there would have been good reason on his side. Four hundred years in Egypt, however harsh, had both succoured my people and sapped their will. They had never had to face the making of a choice, never experienced the hard maturity that comes from having to live with the results of such a choice. So they remained a precarious mixture of superstitious thinking, passionate religious hope and an almost total lack of inner restraint. They had lived as if within a closed eggshell, sustained by the meat provided. To break out of that shell, newly hatched, was to enter an unaccustomed world. To survive, they needed a spirit of independence and strength of will. Observing them, I could see – again, with a chill in my heart – that while the independence was much in evidence, the will was absent. Only a vacillating enthusiasm. Clearly they were going to behave as small children, entitled to safe keeping and a rapid solution to all their problems with but little effort on their own part.

I could see also that were they, at this stage, to encounter an enemy, they would at once lose heart and repent of their journey. It would need only that first alarm, since they were still so freshly fledged, and they would scatter in panic back to the security of Egypt. So I turned them aside, grumbling as they went, yet obedient in default of any other leader. We halted first at Succoth, next at Etham on the fringe of the true desert. And we moved in haste, always fearful lest Pharaoh might pursue us.

For me, as I faced the wilderness once again, there was a release of the spirit, as if the top layer of anxiety had been peeled away. I greeted the vast emptiness as an old, much-loved antagonist. Each stretch of yellow-grey scrub, each desert spring, each gravelled range of hills, unfolded itself before my eyes as if they were a map that had been carefully stored away and retained for this precise occasion. Trembling for my people, as yet so untried, I myself grappled the desert to my heart with thanksgiving. I had come home. My way was open. It was to take me south and east to where the yellow walls of Horeb, far distant and now but a phantom in my mind, awaited my coming.

But it was not I who led the way. This much became clear to me from the beginning. The desert is a strange place and strange things can happen in it. It holds a different kind of reality from other places; it offers, if you will accept it, a different quality of being. Perhaps it is more potent as a condition of mind than as the stones and sand a man will actually tread. There is a desert within each of us. But a desert is not always barren. It can enfold you with a luminous immensity of the spirit. This I had discovered when I knelt before the burning bush. And now, as I led my people towards the mountain, I was under no illusion that it was I who walked at their head. Not I, but the Lord. Always.

For indeed there was That which went before us. Hidden within the pillar of cloud by day, manifested by the pillar of fire by night, It drew us steadily into the reality prepared for us. The Lord was with us, and I walked beside him along the indecipherable desert ways. By day I gazed upon the cloud, towering into the sky as a shaft of pearl. By night I watched the column of fire where it burned into the desert darkness and illumined our passage.

Did I, alone, see It? Or were my people, also, aware of the power that travelled with us? Who am I to belittle their vision? Yet, preoccupied as they were with the hazards of the journey, anxious, even frightened, suffering from the pain of uprooting and pitched into a strange and to them unlovely world, my people had little of themselves to spare for marvels. Indeed, they seemed unable to comprehend the great cloud moving before them over the surface of the desert, staring with indifferent, dust-caked eyes as if it were some simple peculiarity of this inhospitable landscape, some aberrant exhibition of natural forces bringing to those who noticed it a sickening vertigo. I recalled my own avoidance of the burning bush. Let me not see it, I had said. So also they must have whispered to themselves.

At night, camping in huddled exhaustion, or pressing sullenly along the march, they too seemed unable to understand that the steady light which made everything around them as clear as day was not perhaps a quite prosaic happening in this new, extraordinary world. They dropped their eyes before it, unwilling to see, nursing their tiredness, their ill-humour, their sudden angers. Most people, after all, do not wish to be disturbed in their resentments.

But of one thing I could be certain. Aaron, now silent and subdued, recognised the cloud and the fire for what It was. He walked beside me, though a half-step behind, and his face was sombre and afraid. During those days Miriam was no longer with us, having been sent by Aaron back into the rank and file to join her husband. This was because of her growing urge towards power, deprived of which she set herself up as some kind of prophetess, ready to advise us all and thus to grasp authority over us. Even Aaron, swayed by her in Egypt, could now see that her close presence was unwise.

So, behind us, we chose Joshua and Caleb as our runners, and they, in their devotion, built a screen between us and the long rabble of people and carts and protesting animals. Our pace was necessarily accommodated to that of our herds, which meant we moved but slowly – a terrible, frightening slowness which irked us so that at times we lashed the unwilling beasts. Beyond the Sea of Reeds we might count ourselves safe from Pharaoh. Until then we must not rest.

We came down to the sea in early dawn, a still, pale water giving off decay, a closed-in, suffocating marsh smell. It stretched away, heavy with rising heat. I tried to see into the distance, but there was only a soft blanket of mist clinging to the surface of the oily waters. So I hesitated, uneasy at that peculiar flat calm, feeling that something was wrong but unable to tell what it might be.

Little sucking noises were borne in upon me, odd withdrawals of the tide, which then welled up again from beneath the muddy sand. Apart from these yawnings and blowings, small, throttled sounds which increased my disquiet, the water was lifeless. I watched carefully, and saw only those erratic retirements of the tide along the fringes of the sea and the equally sudden uprush of oozing mud which spun back in lazy circles.

Behind me, my people crowded round the baggage train along the shore. Beside me, the Lord's cloud merged into the mist. But then, filtering in across the empty wasteland, I distinguished an excited commotion of voices, muted by distance yet undoubtedly shouts of triumph. There was a drumming of horses, even the sharp clank of armour, and then the grinding of chariot wheels. It could have but one meaning: that Pharaoh had once again repented of his repentance. I buried my face in my hands, weakened at this critical moment by an unguarded uprush of fury against the desert for betraying us. By my side, Joshua dropped to his knees, raising his arms to where the cloud waited. I knew then that, all along, he had recognised That which had led us to this place.

I felt rather than saw the wave of panic that rippled over my people like wind over grass. There was a man – three or four men – heavy and black-bearded, shaking with fear and rage as they left their beasts and rushed upon me. 'Because there were no graves in Egypt,' they clamoured, 'hast thou taken us away to die in the wilderness?' And another, shaking his fist: 'Wherefore hast thou dealt thus with us, to bring us forth out of Egypt?' And yet another, thrusting himself against me and spitting into my face: 'Is not this the word that we spake unto thee in Egypt, saying Let us alone, that we may serve the Egyptians?'

And then a fleshy giant of a man, scowling and afraid: 'Better for us to serve the Egyptians than that we should die in the wilderness.' He flung out his arm in a gesture of repudiation, and the others bellowed their agreement.

And I? I stood before them, my tongue locked in my mouth, acknowledging my impotence.

---- VIII ----

The Horse and His Rider

Now my whole being shivered into pieces, and I heard again the man in Egypt long ago: 'Who made thee a prince and a judge over us?' I, the simple herdsman, having set myself up to be the mouthpiece of the Lord, and now discovered, as before, to be of no account. Capable of magic manipulation. Able to conjure up a morsel of shape-shifting. No more. Just the illusions of an empty trickster, when what was now needed, were we to be saved, was the Lord's own miracle to redeem his people.

No wonder they bludgeoned me with their anger. I, walking proudly beside the pillar of cloud, assuming the garments of leadership, but now devoid of power and no longer a suitable vessel. I stared around me as a doomed beast frozen in its tracks, while the cries came nearer out of the mist, and the boy Joshua sprang to his feet and Aaron stepped sideways biting his lip and the men stood glowering in their terror at the rising tumult.

Then, with amazement, I heard my own voice. Strange, how quiet it sounded, although it reached to the edges of our people. 'Fear ye not,' I told them, gently, as to very young children, my tongue loosed and speaking the words of comfort. 'Stand still, and see the salvation of the Lord, which he will work for you today: for the Egyptians whom ye have seen today . . .' – and indeed there were shapes now looming out of the distance –' . . . ye shall see them no more for ever.'

I turned from them, finding an unexpected certainty within myself. 'The Lord shall fight for you,' I added, 'and ye shall hold your peace.'

Then I stood before the sea, as the voice of the Lord came to me out of the centre of the cloud. 'Lift up your rod,' I was told, 'and stretch out thine hand over the sea, and divide it: and the children of Israel shall go into the midst of the sea on dry ground.'

I did as I was instructed, standing with uplifted arms and my staff held stiffly, pointing a way through the waters. I remember nothing of the words I used. Only that I asked the Lord for our necessary miracle, and that I requested the sea to abandon its habitual place. Also that I offered myself as an unworthy sacrifice, should such be required, to be obliterated in the waters if, by so doing, my people might cross in safety.

It seemed that the whole of creation was stilled as we waited for the waters to be obedient. I remember the huge form of the malakh as it went, slowly, before the moving pillar of cloud and stood with it between us and the advancing chariots. I heard the dismayed confusion of Pharaoh's people.

Then, suddenly, came the sea's response, as the tide quaked and shrank. From beneath the waters I heard an explosive sucking as of a gigantic indrawn breath, a fearful suffocation as the sea drew back. It vanished secretly, drawn down into a myriad small mud-holes in the quivering sea-bed. And finally there came a terrible sound – a long, strangled moaning – as it drained away, far off, far down.

A flat, rough bridge of sand was now revealed, thick with weeds and rushes lying spent upon their sides. At first sight of it, we still could not move, standing as if made of stone. The cloud was behind us, its darkness a shelter, and the voice of the Lord called to me again: 'Speak unto the children of Israel, that they go forward.'

So I spoke to them and the spell was broken, and they hurled themselves across the causeway in a frenzy to reach the other bank, the carts heaving and creaking under the strain, the women and children pushing and pulling, the men savagely lashing the crazed, struggling herds of animals.

But at last it was done. I alone was left, standing before the pathway, powerless to move, and waiting. Humbly? That seemed doubtful. Gladly? No, that was too much to ask. I knew only that I had to be there, should the sacrifice be exacted. In that moment I saw myself small, a tiny speck of being contained in a single droplet of the sea. I noted my still divided mind, and all my insufficiencies, my unquelled arrogance and my posture of meekness. Perhaps it was right that I should be taken. Perhaps – but the drop of water rose in a bubble of light and burst against the sun, leaving me as I had been before. Untouched. The rejected offering. Certainly no substitute victim, heroically redeeming my people.

I looked around me as one drunk and unseeing, floundering a little as I set off across the sand-bridge, obstinately holding my staff aloft as if that action itself could hold the waters back, and conscious that both Caleb and Joshua were supporting my rigid arms. I went slowly, knowing that the pillar of cloud moved with me, and when I reached the far shore, I turned and knelt before It. And all my people, as if their sight had been rinsed clean, knelt also and worshipped.

As in a dream I looked out and saw the horses, saw Pharaoh's chariots racing across the sand-bridge, saw how some of them hung back in the middle while others came on, saw how the chariot wheels stuck and broke, heard the shouts of terror as at last they understood that the Lord God of Israel was fighting against them to redeem his first-born.

And then I was called upon to end it. I had known that this would be, and I shrank from it. Yet once more, with my heart tired and my mind sick, I raised my rod to call the waters back. They came, the waves returning in a vast thunder, and sweeping every stick and stone from their path.

I watched, unblinking, because I must not flinch. I stared with a dreadful detachment, and soon the sea had covered the chariots and the horsemen so that there remained not one of them left.

After it was over I fell on my face on the muddy bank and wept. But the cloud stood beside me, tall and unmoving and unmoved, and when I rose to my feet, I saw at a distance that Joshua was squatting in the rank grass, watching me closely and biting his thumb. He came and stood at my shoulder as I ordered my people to make camp.

It was when we had fed our beasts, and eaten our own meal, and when the thick mist had cleared away and the sun burned fully down upon us, that I heard the jubilation and, looking up, saw Miriam leading the women in a dance of thanksgiving. They had timbrels in their hands and they sang wildly and ecstatically. Miriam's voice rose and fell in a fierce shout of mastery: 'Sing ye to the Lord, for he hath triumphed gloriously. The horse and his rider hath he thrown into the sea.'

I watched in silence. Well, they needed their release and if they gloated, Miriam whipping them into an unseemly fervour, who was I to halt them?

Yet I felt diminished by a deep and bitter sorrow, and as I stood there, seeing yet not seeing, there drifted across my vision a small group of black-robed men, seated not outside our crowded tents but with a shimmering shape of walls and windows about them. They were strange to me, not in any way resembling the Israelite herdsmen standing at the edge of the dance and fiercely clapping out the rhythm. But it was upon those well-accustomed forms that this quiet group was impressed.

Then a voice sounded within my mind, and suddenly I understood what they were, those gentle teachers from a time far into the future, as they expounded the happenings of this day which was for them far back in their own ancient past.

'The ministering angels', came the precise and thoughtful voice, 'were about to chant songs of praise as the Egyptians were drowning, but the Almighty rebuked them with the words *My people are perishing in the sea – and will ye sing?'*

Here I strode into the throng of dancers, raising my arms on high and cutting into their elation with what sounded, even to my own ears, a dreadful, savage, lonely cry. Are you higher than the angels? I demanded. Can you not hear the Lord's rebuke? And then I shouted the words which had come to me from that other time: '*My people are perishing in the sea – and will ye sing?'*

I stood among them. Gone now were those old, quiet men. The singing jarred to a whisper, my people eyeing me askance with a stunned lack of comprehension. Then, all at once, they surged forward, still refusing to understand, forming great circles about me, shouting my name and praising me.

But I stayed in the midst of them, crying like a child, my head bowed and my tears trickling into my beard. And very soon, as they whirled about me, singing and laughing and beating their instruments, I felt a touch upon my arm. It was Joshua, looking grave and many years older than his youth, who led me as a blind man away into the silence of my tent.

IX

The Coin of Our Release

Yet I went out to my people and joined in the singing.

Why? Because, unwilling, I knew that this was what I had to do. But first, and for a long time, I crouched on a stool in my tent, rubbing my hands over and over my knees.

Did I so love the Egyptians that I could not bear to see them destroyed? No. This I had to admit. Even though I myself had been treated in Egypt with courtesy – indeed, at times with terrified respect – I needed only to remember the suffering of my people to know where my choice must lie. My despair came because choice was implicit in the situation, and death seemed a dreary waste. I remembered the first-born, and Pharaoh's dereliction. I heard the chariot wheels breaking in the Sea of Reeds. Our own safety had been purchased at a heavy price. By others. So I could not feel jubilant, and, left to myself, would have spent the aftermath of that destruction in silence. But I was not.

For it had been impossible, even as I had been led, grieving, to my tent, not to remark the frozen look on Joshua's face, and the downcast eyes of Caleb, both of them sullen, embarrassed, withdrawn. Was I a suitable leader? Or merely a straw figure easily vanquished by tears and sentiment? Now, hidden from their condemnation, I had no answer. I thought about Caleb, acknowledging his eagerness, his shrewd judgements, even while still a boy and in these early days of our wandering. I considered the merits of Joshua and knew a quick rush of certainty. For in Joshua I could recognise the future commander of our people: fierce, loyal, uncompromising, clear-minded – a Joshua passionately in love with his God. Neither Caleb nor Joshua would flinch from the present wild rejoicing, the sound now beating agains the wall of my tent, so that I could distinguish, through the leather flaps, the roar of voices uplifted in homage to a God of wrath, bloody and victorious.

'The Lord is a man of war,' they chanted, 'Thy right hand, O Lord, dasheth in pieces the enemy. . . .'

Well, should they not rejoice? I was seized by an idea which seemed strange and might even imply the Lord's inadequacy: could the Lord do other than work his deliverance at the level of wisdom we, his children, had attained? Or did this limit his power? Or, rather, did he limit himself because those he had created were limited? Men expect an invincible God, one who will chastise and, if need be, destroy; one who will pour down his anger, querulous and hot-tempered, and will readily draw his sword in vengeance. For their sake, of course, and, naturally, against other people. Perhaps we are shown the God we desire. Perhaps he can – will – reveal himself to us only in a guise we are able to accept.

This seemed to me important. In the short time since we had left Egypt I had discovered not simply that my people were feckless and intractable, but that they responded only to harsh and unremitting discipline. Four hundred years of slave labour had, as I had already suspected, sufficiently warped their minds that all they now answered to was either a magical solution that would immediately end their problems, or another kind of oppression would leave them no opportunity to rebel.

Where in all this, I wondered, was there room for the silence of God? For his patient gentleness? For his infinite, appalling, compassionate humility? (That he should choose me. That he was ready to speak through my ignorance.) And how, I asked myself, might I, this stammering mouthpiece, so direct my people's fluctuating attention that the Lord God of Israel possessed them entirely within his heart?

Reluctantly, with chilled vision, I saw that the Lord's wrath was inescapable, even that his vengeance might ultimately descend upon his own chosen. The Lord, I told myself, was darkness as well as light. And just as we, his creatures, faced darkness in the world around us, that darkness had to be included within his all-embracing Being. If the dark and the light were not both contained within him, then he could not be the One Lord of the universe.

I saw, too, that out of this perverse, unstable people, there had to be forged the instrument, not of God's wrath but of his wisdom. To be his presence on the earth. Also, that in the making there would be breaking. This I shrank from but had to accept. And perhaps the instrument of grace that my people must become might not be perfected in our own generation, since the time of the Lord might well be other than the time we ourselves have constructed.

Struggling with these ideas, I tried also to envisage who would bear the reckoning, if such there had to be, of our inevitable backsliding; who would take upon himself the burden of inadequacy and sin? It might be that I myself, and I shrank from the idea, even though housing the fire of the Lord's spirit, might also become the scapegoat of God: the inarticulate, the impotent, who would be responsible for my people's wrong-doing and who, in the end, would be forsaken in the desert. Or would it be the Lord himself who would bear this burden?

It seemed that I was caught between the nether and the upper millstones. There was the need for mastering my people so that they became obedient to the Lord, though even he might find the task unrewarding. Perhaps compliance would be won only when their obduracy met with the greater obduracy of the Lord. Perhaps, in order to ensure their total sanctification, the Lord had first to break their mulish will; if need be, inexorably to shut the gates of his mercy. I shuddered at the possibility of any such implacable dealing.

This dark necessity would be the heavy, unrelenting burden of the Lord's displeasure. But above his wrath and tempering its violence would brood an unfathomable promise, perhaps a matter beyond comprehension for a slave people, however steeped in age-long belief. This was that aspect of the Lord which I held within myself, so much at variance with chastisement. I saw a God who grieved over his people, extending his attentiveness to all mankind. He was the one inescapable, incontestable Lord God of Israel, beyond malice, beyond anger, beyond retribution. It would be the Lord's task – my task – to implant such a notion into his as yet untamed, impetuous people. For I could see that this journey was not only towards a Promised Land but towards a Promised People.

And through it all I recognised with apprehension that the darkness and the blood would be there. Because we were human. The blood of the first-born, the drowning of the Egyptian host, both were a part of that darkness. And here, I even began, painfully, to understand that there is a price set to everything in this life, and that we have to be prepared to pay that price. Some are not prepared to pay it. Some are not prepared that the price should be paid for them by others. I even saw, as a stain on the horizon, our coming battles as we advanced through tribal territories towards the Promised Land: no miracles achieved by the Lord's intervention but fought by my people hand to hand and sword to sword. There would be death then, whoever the initiator, and those deaths would be the dark side of the coin.

And I foresaw the rejoicing over these deaths, the human emotions of envy and wrath, the human acts of riot and destruction. And these emotions would, by reference, be accredited to the Lord God of Israel, since we see in our God the attributes we ourselves find necessary.

I saw a long chronicle unfolding, stretching into the centuries, a chronicle of human fallibility as well as of the Lord's dealings with his people. And, moreover, a reading into the Lord's admonishments of emotions which the Lord himself might not have intended, yet which he would inscrutably acknowledge because he worked within his children's insufficiencies. They would all – these misconceptions of the Lord's enigmatic nature – be part of the price, the heavy price, to be paid for our continuing devotion. And this would not be understood by those who came later. So that, in spite of our devotion, the Lord God would also be involved in the cost. He also would pay. He also would offer himself. But then of course he would have been aware of this risk from the beginning.

The Lord's payment had already begun. Not back in the time of our patriarchs when he established us as a people. But in this present time, when he laid the foundation of our faith. From the moment when he approached me in the burning bush, ready to use my weaknesses as well as my strengths, the Lord God had entered his humanity in such a way that he became, of his own choice and volition, actively involved in the process of suffering and in the reconciliation.

I thought about this, seeing more clearly what my own part must be. Sitting there, in the tent's soft filtered light, I reached, for a time at least, a kind of tranquillity, a still point between one pole and the other. Perhaps, I told myself, I would ultimately encompass this strange mission, so that, while I might not always (or even often) manage to control my intractable people, my inadequacy would not matter. Perhaps the Lord knew all this, had known it all along. Perhaps it was not such a vast mistake that he had made, out there in the desert, when he spoke to me from the burning bush.

I raised my head and listened. But there was no response. Only the shadow of the cloud across my tent, bringing coolness.

X

The Right Hand of the Lord

So at length I rose from my stool, knowing that I must go out to my people and that I must not alienate them or forfeit the sudden uprush of allegiance I had this day aroused. I must be, yes, as cunning as the desert serpent, so that I did not lose them, in derision at what they would see as my weakness, to Aaron's hungry pride and Miriam's disruptiveness. I must – but could I? – tread delicately upon the knife-edge between what my people could bear and what I would eventually teach them. The go-between, guarding my own inner stability – if I were able. There would come the time when my voice must thunder, but that time was not yet, and for now my people had to be cosseted a little, borne with and cajoled, not faced too bleakly with more than they could endure.

I thought with rapture of those gentle, pacific scholars – also my people yet perfected in charity in a time far beyond this present chaos. I must not – indeed, I could not – force their wisdom upon my own generation.

I went out then from my tent and saw that I had been wise to do so. Aaron's sudden glance, and the two spots of high colour on his cheekbones, were always signs of repressed anger. And there was Miriam, exuding triumph as she led her almost worshipping women and received the tributes and admiration of the men. In that moment I could see that I had nearly lost them.

The people were singing in a shrill, high, passionate glorification of the Lord's victory. 'Pharaoh's chariots and his host hath he cast into the sea,' they exulted, repeating endlessly the phrases of death. (Yet had they not so narrowly escaped from bondage?) I, too, joined in the words though implying, from a sombre heart, something different. 'The deeps cover them: they went down into the depths like a stone. Thy right hand, O Lord, is glorious in power, thy right hand, O Lord, dasheth in pieces the enemy.'

As they chanted the fearful words, the dancing slowed to a halt, and now a queer, strained silence came over them, though their voices still throbbed within me in a savage chord. Thy right hand, O Lord. . . . Thy right hand. . . . Is that how they saw me? The instrument of God? Glorious in power? The silence spread rapidly as men, women and even small children stood in huddled groups, eyeing me warily as if waiting to see what I would do, waiting for me to act.

But I, too, was silent, awkward now, my tongue stiff and useless. I felt a choked panic as the moments slipped away and I made no move. Knowing I was expected to take command. Knowing that I could not – could never – assert myself. Knowing that the recognition must come from them.

Then suddenly, as I stood there in my sickness and indecision, a wave of movement broke on the edges of the nearest crowd. They rushed upon me, shouting boisterously, clutching at my robe. A group of young men hoisted me shoulder-high, forging a way through the now wildly yelling host. They placed me upon a makeshift platform and, like bees around a queen, my people swarmed about me.

I looked down. I saw their upturned faces – I, raised above them and meeting, with a leap of exultation, the great wash of praise and thanksgiving that rose and broke like a giant wave upon me.

Exultation? Yes. This I must acknowledge. A strange, intoxicating birth. Trembling, I shrank from it with horrified revulsion, yet it also flowed like wine through every crevice of my being. I was filled with their roaring, struck dumb by their passion, threatened by the power of their elation.

'. . . Thou sendest forth thy wrath, it consumeth them as stubble. And with the blast of thy nostrils, the waters were piled up, the floods stood upright as an heap; the deeps were congealed in the heart of the sea.'

The words pulled at me, so that I was nothing but a small unaccountable thing, borne on the torrent of jubilation. Even Aaron shouted with the rest, while Miriam's hair, unbound, whipped about her as she leapt and beat her timbrels.

'Thou didst blow with thy wind, the sea covered them: they sank as lead in the mighty waters. . . .'

And then with a hoarse bellow of acclaim, partly for the Lord and partly, as I could see, for his right hand: 'Who is like unto thee, O Lord, among the gods? Who is like thee, glorious in holiness, fearful in praises, doing wonders? Thou stretchedst out thy right hand, the earth swallowed them.'

I was standing with my back to the Sea of Reeds, facing east and south to where the mountain of Horeb waited for me, deep in the shadowy distance. I watched, on an overwhelming tide of vanity, my own lean, banished self, crossing those stony wastes – I, the cloven-tongued outcast who yet had been chosen to house the fire of God, to reveal himself as the messenger, to become the Lord's mouthpiece.

For a moment, as my people crowded about me (*my* people? Should I not say the Lord's people?) I tasted the unreliable sweetness of their acclaim. The outcast, now recognised (. . . that flicker of reckless delight). The acknowledged leader (. . . that fiery draught of power). Dangerous? Indeed. Something, I tried to tell myself, to be kept in balance, without damage either to them or to myself.

Yet, dazed with elation, I ignored my own danger. Instead, as I looked out across the sea of faces below me, I felt myself to be an eagle, daring the mountain skies and riding the treacherous currents of the desert air.

Well, it did not last. For even I, raised so violently to such unwonted heights, and shouting now with my people in a kind of ecstasy, knew that those currents of light-minded flattery could change in a moment, dropping me like a stone.

'The Lord is my strength. . . .' I struggled to articulate, my people joining me as their bodies swayed rhythmically back and forth, 'and he is become my salvation: this is my God, and I will praise him; my father's God, and I will exalt him.'

And now the temper of the host had subtly changed, their song not solely of blood, for presently the ready refrain – 'Thou sendest forth thy wrath' – altered to a more simple, trusting avowal: 'Thou in thy mercy', they sang, their tired voices rippling away into the waiting desert, 'hast led the people which thou hast redeemed. . . .'

I heard my own voice take the lead, and was aware that Miriam's strident cries had died away: '. . . Thou hast guided them in thy strength to thy holy habitation.'

I was conscious now of the pillar of cloud behind me, conscious of vitality pouring into me. I raised my arms above my people as they hid their faces from me.

'Thou shalt bring them in,' I cried to the veiled presence of the Lord, 'and plant them in the mountain of thine inheritance, the place, O Lord, which thou hast made for thee to dwell in, the sanctuary, O Lord, which thy hands have established.'

There came a gentle murmuring from the bended people, a sigh of childlike submission. They raised their heads, gazing not at the pillar of cloud but at the mouthpiece of the Lord, as I said to them, my tongue now clear and unfaltering: 'The Lord is my strength and my song.'

So I came back into myself. But only partly. For the seed of self-glory, lying dormant so long, had been given life, I being unused to its potency.

──── XI ────

The Seventh Day

We moved out of our camp within a few days. In their docile simplicity, the people perhaps imagined we had but a short journey before the Promised Land was to be spread out at our feet.

We entered the wilderness of Shur, already so well known to me that my heart lifted when I saw again that bleak wasteland of sand and stones. I felt I was returned to my true home. Aaron and I, followed closely by Caleb and Joshua, walked at the head of our long caravan. Behind us, the men strode out eagerly, the women veiled themselves against the sun and the children scrambled restlessly over the awkward, rolling carts. Our beasts moved in clouds of dust and flies, plunging and snorting as we crossed the limestone ridges, dropping down into dry, stony water-courses where only a little scrub could be found for them to eat.

Before us, the great pillar of cloud led ever deeper into the wilderness, and often, when I looked back, it seemed to me that the vast, straggling column of our people lay like a gigantic shadow, cast by the cloud across the desert sands.

But even as the wilderness had tested my own raw inexperience, so it tested this unpractised host. They had little time to spare for the arid beauty of parched rock, still less for the soft violet outlines of distant hills, or for the marvel that tamarisk and acacia could send out living branches in such a wasteland. Understandably, their minds were upon essentials: water and food. It took us three days to traverse the strip of desert that led to the spring of Marah, three days without sufficient water and with the people murmuring in discontent and then in panic. 'What shall we drink?' they cried, and the cry became a thunder as we reached Marah's bitter waters, polluted and undrinkable, and stared down at the great pool that had appeared so inviting. At first I despaired, but then, together with our two runners, I found and cut down branches of a thick-leaved tree, the powers of which I had learned to know in the wilderness, and cast them into the waters. After a time, absorbing the bitterness, they left a sweeter water to drink.

I admit I was exasperated, and my tongue lashed out agreeably in a blast of anger as I castigated the people for their fears of contamination and consequent disease. 'If thou wilt diligently hearken to the voice of the Lord thy God . . .' – I spoke testily, so that 'if' became 'if *only*' – '. . . and wilt do that which is right in his eyes, and wilt give ear to his commandments, and keep all his statutes, I (the Lord hath said) will put none of the diseases upon thee, which I have put upon the Egyptians. . . .'

I looked around me at the sheepish crowd kneeling beside the pool and filling their water pots. They were hot and desperately tired, and they were frightened. So I spoke more gently: '. . . I (the Lord hath said) am the Lord that healeth thee.'

Afterwards we came to Elim, where there were twelve springs of water, sufficient for all our families, and the green shade of threescore and ten palm trees. We camped thankfully, and I felt encouraged at having subdued my people a little.

We journeyed from Elim on the fifteenth day of the second month after our departure from Egypt, along a route which was desolate but which my own solitary feet would have gladly trod. And here even Aaron, hitherto majestically distanced from what he considered material trifles, received the concentrated antagonism of our people. The women were the most petulant, their eyes dark with fear as they clasped their children defiantly to their breasts. I was reminded of Zipporah, so that I became fierce again, out of guilt and helplessness.

'Would that we had died by the hand of the Lord,' shrilled the women tearfully, 'in the land of Egypt, when we sat by the flesh-pots, when we did eat bread to the full.' They stroked their children's distended bellies, accusing us bitterly, frightened now not of thirst, for there was plenty of water, but at having no food. 'For ye have brought us forth into the wilderness,' they railed angrily, 'to kill this whole community with hunger!'

There was reason in what they said and, seeing it, the Lord was swift to provide, so that we received the miracle of the quails and the manna. Miracle? Again I questioned that word, knowing from my own experience how, at evening in the desert, there might often come a thick fluttering of birds, falling out of heaven to cover the sandy waste as a feathered carpet – and easily netted. Also I had tasted of the tamarisk tree when its resin had dried into white flour-like wafers and fallen to the ground. But still I repeated the Lord's magical, enheartening words: 'The Lord shall give you in the evening flesh to eat, and in the morning bread to the full.'

They listened, disbelieving, but they rejoiced when the promise came true. So I instructed them in the way the manna should be gathered and milled. Indeed, it was beautiful to see how, in the early dawn, when the dew had gone up, there lay upon the ground a small, round thing, thin and rough and white in colour. It tasted like honey-cake and was duplicated by thousands upon thousands. It was, I knew quite certainly, the only bread we should find throughout our whole long journey to the Promised Land, and quite soon the easy wonder of it would pall. But for the moment it was a strange new delicacy, conjured, it seemed, out of the dry desert soil.

And on the sixth day, as the women smiled, and the children busily gathered this peculiar substance, the Lord spoke to me, so that, suddenly prompted, I made them gather sufficient manna for the following day also. 'Tomorrow is a solemn rest,' I explained to them, 'a holy sabbath unto the Lord.' And I went on to direct them as to how they should prepare their meat and the flour-wafers in advance: 'Bake that which ye will bake, and seethe that which you will seethe; and all that remaineth over lay up for you to be kept until the morning.'

Watching them at work on that sixth day, I knew a deep content. On the next day my people would rest, doing no labour. And this would be a pattern in their lives for the future – the six days of toil and the seventh day of recreation which they would give entirely to the Lord. I could see it established in a rhythm of worship extending throughout all the generations of the Lord's people: that day of easeful prayer set aside for their God.

'Thou shalt call the Sabbath a delight,' I whispered to myself, though I had not even thought these words, 'and the holy day of the Lord honourable.'

The words bore into me, and it was at this moment of foreknowledge that I went away by myself, finding a place where the pool beside which we were camped was bounded by a stony outcrop. I squatted beneath a palm tree, staring down into the water, dazzled by the patches of sun and shadow that flickered over the surface. Presently I forgot both the place and the distant noises of the camp, gazing blankly through the shifting mosaic of light and dark until I came to a room where a woman was standing before me. She was pale of complexion and dark-eyed, looking straight at me as if in recognition. Yet, like the young man in the darkness of Egypt, she did not see me.

It was a strange room, with people curiously dressed, and a covered table with plaited bread and silver candlesticks, before which the woman raised her hands in benediction. 'Lord of the Universe,' she said, in a tongue I knew, though it was not easy to follow, 'I am about to perform the sacred duty of kindling the lights in honour of the Sabbath, even as it is written. . . .' And here she repeated the words which, earlier, I had so involuntarily used: 'And thou shalt call the Sabbath a delight, and the holy day of the Lord honourable.'

The prayer beat against my mind as, carefully, with her lips composed gently one against the other and her eyes quiet, the woman lit the waiting candles. Then she blessed them.

The waters rippled to and fro and the scene below me faded and sharpened and faded again. I heard a man's voice, telling that the children of Israel would keep the Sabbath throughout their generations, for an everlasting covenant. I heard a thanksgiving that the Lord our God had brought forth bread and wine out of the earth.

Kneeling now, and peering through the water, I had yet again a sense of being outside time – that this was so far into our unimaginable future that I could not even envisage it; that millennia must have passed and that now, in this unknown house and by these unknown people, this Sabbath day was being sanctified which I, under the Lord's guidance and in this earlier time, had begun to establish.

The waters shivered into fragments of sunlight and I came back into myself. So. Did it matter that this present time would be difficult? Did it matter that my people were sometimes obstinate and often truculent? Eventually, even if long past my day, the Lord would be continually sanctified within the people of Israel.

They, the whole people, throughout the whole of time, would be his messenger, would house his spirit – they, the mouthpiece of the One God.

I rose to my feet, giddy as the dark brightness struck against me.

XII

The March to Horeb

The first of those endless battles that hampered our passage through the desert came at Rephidim, when the Amalekites descended upon us. They were a wild and vicious people, always to be our avowed enemy. The attack took us by surprise when we were resting after a long march, so that before night brought a merciful halt to the fighting we had lost many who had been weak and over-weary even before the battle.

It was then that I gave Joshua his chance. 'Choose us out men,' I ordered, 'and go out, fight with Amalek.'

Then an idea came to me, one which I felt was harmless but would give my people courage. 'Tomorrow,' I told him, making it seem an undertaking of some consequence, so that the news would spread rapidly, 'I shall stand on the top of the hill with the rod of God in mine hand.'

This I did, as the desert sun came up next morning, striking directly into the faces of the enemy and blinding them, much to our advantage. On one side of me, I placed Aaron, and on the other – a careful choice – Hur, the husband of Miriam. Hur was a plain man, simple in his ways and without guile. In his forbearance, he was quite unable to control that obstructive sister of mine, but it seemed to me I should be wise to keep him constantly at my side, that I might the better have an open ear to Miriam's various deceptions.

Joshua had chosen well and with the desert helping us we began to gain over the Amalekites. Long after, it would be said that when I boldly threatened, with my rod held high, then Israel prevailed, while, if my hand faltered as I grew weary, Amalek gained in strength.

But there was rather more to it than that. This was our first encounter with an enemy, and my people were only too aware of the urgency of our cause. Perhaps this served to bind us together: myself and the fighting men and those who watched fearfully from behind the carts and tents. At any rate, it seemed almost as if we were fused into one being, delicately responsive, as one organism, either to hope or despair, swaying easily between both. I sensed that I, on my hilltop, was the force directing this pliable, common mind, so that what I did there could charge it with energy, or, conversely, sap all confidence. So it was true: when my rod was high, they responded with fresh heart, but when, in exhaustion, my arms drooped to my sides, I knew that power had gone out of them.

As the day wore on, and the fighting ebbed and flowed between our two hosts, I became less and less able to stand with my rod raised. At length Aaron and Hur rolled forward a large rock so that I could sit, and they stationed themselves one on each side of me, holding my arms up when my strength faltered, as Caleb and Joshua had supported them crossing the Sea of Reeds. In this way, the rod was kept steady till the sun went down.

I suppose this very ordinary rod must have appeared to the people as a rallying-point, sacred because the Lord had frequently acted through it, an emblem into which they poured their faith and from which they derived vitality, and which they might not humiliate. I wished it had been a more dramatic and encouraging talisman, such as a piece of rich weaving made into a banner, and it was while I was thinking such thoughts, the sun now westering and bright against my eyes, that for a single moment I seemed to glimpse just such a banner blazing over Joshua and his men.

Strange that it should be there, I thought, a symbol unknown to me, the device of a blue star, its six points imprinted on a white ground, shimmering yet transparent in the pull of the desert wind. Look! I found myself shouting, do you see it? The Shield of David! Fighting for us! Then I fell silent, ashamed of the nonsense I had spoken and thinking myself overcome by fatigue. For, even as I watched, the banner was gone. Aaron, it seemed, had not even heard me, merely shrugging, while Hur gazed blankly. But Joshua was victorious. The Amalekites gave back before his sword, and those of them who remained alive fled away across the desert.

We did not follow them, and I descended the hill to build an altar on which to offer the sacrifice of our thanksgiving. I knew without doubt that we would have war against Amalek from generation to generation, and I sorrowed over this, but I knew also that I could not change what was to be.

After this, we made our way without hindrance to Mount Horeb. It took longer than a week, since many were wounded and this meant several halts along the way, that they might be lifted from the carts and tended more conveniently in our tents.

I was glad of our slow progress. On this march I drew ever away from my companions, striding with a measured pace that ate up the miles. Aaron was left far behind with Hur, and both Caleb and Joshua had a hard time of it acting as intermediaries between me and my people.

But I craved the solitude. Using a practised tread, each footfall barely lifting the dusty sand, and with my sun-dazed eyes fixed ever on the rising buttresses of Horeb, I felt I must accomplish this journey in silence. Mile after yellow mile, ridge upon stony ridge, gully after dry gully, it was the way of contentment, with the load of my people's clamour left far behind. I thought, as I moved south into the back of the wilderness, that this was a time of preparation. A time to quieten the spirit, to open out the mind. I looked into the future, not knowing what it might bring, but aware that there was something which awaited me, something which I would have to do.

As the tiny spirals of sand funnelled up along the open desert, roused by a gathering wind, I saw Mount Horeb as becoming the seat of majesty. I remembered those days in our ancient past when the whole of creation – yes, even this parched desert – had come into being as the Lord crooked his finger. That was the old beginning, when he divided the light from the darkness, and made the firmament and gave us evening and morning and gathered up the waters. But this – this that awaited us – would be the new beginning. Because on Mount Horeb, and the thought took shape within me, the Lord would reveal himself to his people.

Halting for a moment beside a dried-up bush (no, not my burning bush, though just such another, and were not all bushes holy?), I felt a sense of revelation, as if I had known all along that here would be our true meeting-place, that place where we, the

— 72 —

people of Israel, would plight our troth with our God. And had the Lord, when he brought into being that earth which then was waste and void, perhaps lovingly arranged the rocks of Mount Horeb, knowing it would be in that place where he would bind his people to him?

And now, as Horeb loomed vastly across the desert, and as I rejoiced over the blue-shadowed valleys cleft into its side, saluting its yellow walls and the huge ramparts of its summit, I remembered the words spoken to me by the Lord out of the burning bush, when I had been so doubtful of my ability to bring my people out of Egypt. 'Certainly I shall be with thee,' he had told me, in a voice so tender that his compassion ran through my veins, 'and this shall be the token unto thee, that I have sent thee: when thou hast brought forth the people out of Egypt, ye shall serve God upon this mountain.'

I turned his words over again in my mind. Here, I was to minister to the Lord God of Israel. Here, my people were to be given a sign, leaving no possible doubt as to – what? My own supremacy? Was that still what I secretly cherished? No, I told myself. Even though the Lord had also said that in the sight of Egypt, and also for Aaron, I would be as God (and even though my heart had leapt a little), yet I might not take any glory to myself. Rather be struck down in the desert, scorched to a cinder in the Lord's fire. Rather be turned – and a small chill licked about me – from entering the Land he had promised us. Had I come all this way, I chided myself, only to yield to my own weaknesses? I shivered under the hot sun. Let me resist myself, O Lord, I whispered. I know my temptation and I fear it.

Alone for a few moments in a scrub-filled ravine, I fell to my knees, the cloud before me, immense and still. I stared up at the Presence, at its soft, luminous, veiled protection. And it was as if I heard the breath of a voice saying: 'Come up to me into the mount, and be there.'

There was nothing more, only the whip of the rising wind and the clatter of stones as Joshua appeared over the ridge and jarred to a halt. I rose and climbed the other side of the gully, again keeping my distance.

During those last few days of the approach to Horeb I debated many practical matters, trying to hold a balance between what I felt to be my own desire for a disciplined remoteness and the certainty that I must be available to my people. For now, whenever we made camp, there were long streams of petitioners, seeking me out and demanding my verdict on all their problems. They brought me their quarrels, their ailments, their dealings with one another. They clamoured for justice in the ordering of their households, in their rights over their beasts, in the precedence which each company sought to wrest from the other. I was expected, during the long hours of their wrangling, to give sentence over every dispute, to restore equity to every claimant. I, the judge, the lawgiver, the guide, the prophet, the leader of this tempestuous host over which I appeared now to have charge.

Once I said to them, despairing of the long tail of supplicants each day, yet in what I hoped was a playful good humour (though I am not good at that, and they know it): 'The Lord, the God of your fathers, make you a thousand times so many more as ye are, and bless you, as he hath promised you!'

But, like children, they hated ambiguity, and in the end I turned away, adding wearily (though out of their hearing lest they felt abandoned): 'How can I myself alone bear your cumbrance, and your burden, and your strife?'

Judge, leader, prophet. . . . Where in all this domestic argument might I remain that messenger, housing the fire of the spirit, which the Lord had called me to be? Once, I spoke with Aaron about my dilemma, but he merely looked at me as if I were an oddity and not quite in charge of myself. I understood then that it was not wise to let anyone see my perplexity. The shrewd glint in Aaron's eyes told me that neither he nor they would have mercy over weakness. I had seen animals so behave when one of the flock was born malformed. There would be a trampling, and then the flock was clean. . . .

XIII

Jethro

So we came to Mount Horeb and pitched our tents in that same wide valley where in my exile I had grazed my sheep. But there was a small encampment already in possession, compact and in good order, giving unmistakable evidence of people long acquainted with desert ways. I saw a gaunt, white-haired man, a younger woman and two young men. When I looked again at the older man, my heart gave a great lurch of joy, for here at last was the friend and counsellor I needed – Jethro, my father-in-law, in whom I might confide. But when I took stock of the woman, my heart misgave me, for it was Zipporah – an older, more composed, yet still resentful wife who had brought me my two young sons.

Well, surely I could have been kind? For at least she had made the journey when she might have stayed with her sisters. But I received her coldly. Did not the years spent with Jethro rather than with me, her husband, give me the right to deal with her as a wilful chattel? Whatever the rights of it, and though I have been at fault, I could no longer brook her moodiness. It was, I decided, too late to turn back. She had changed during those years, having built a complacent armour against tenderness. I, too, had changed. I saw it in the flinching look she gave me, judging me now as grey and grim-visaged, a man set apart, not to be trifled with or manipulated (or so I told myself). Her dull flush of greeting signalled aversion, and, with no remorse, I sent her to the women, not taking her into my own tent and making the reason clear in the formality of my dismissal. That she would go to Miriam was inevitable and this, I knew, boded ill, so that any chance of reconciliation vanished as Zipporah defiantly gathered up her skirts and, turning from me, loosed on Miriam a transfiguring smile of sisterly regard.

But the boys I kept with me: Gershom, my eldest, 'the stranger' as I had cruelly named him out of my own loneliness, and Eliezer, that 'help of God' whom I decided, together with his brother, to keep under my own care. Did they resent me? I could not tell, though I hoped that whatever Zipporah had instilled into them about their father, might have been softened by Jethro's influence.

But first, under the shadow of Horeb and before I concerned myself with my wife and my sons, I saluted Jethro. And to him I made obeisance. There, before all my inquisitive people, I dropped to my knees before him, laying my head upon his shoes. The dust blew into my mouth, and Jethro's heavy garments swung about me, but still I knelt there, clasping his feet and knowing a moment of surprised and inexpressible peace, as if I had returned home to my father's house. At length I asked for his blessing, feeling his hands shake as they gentled my rough head. But his voice was as firm as in time past, holding still that loving warmth which had power, always, to melt my stubborn heart.

So, as I knelt there, it was seen by my people that Jethro, the priest of Midian, was a man of consequence to whom veneration must be given. Even Aaron, ever watchful over his own interests, came and stood nearby, calculating, as I could judge, that the visit would not last long and that a show of courtesy could do little to damage his own pride of place.

When the blessing had been given, Jethro raised me and folded me to him. 'I, thy father-in-law-Jethro,' he said, and his voice was loving, 'am come unto thee.'

He turned to where Zipporah stood with chin fiercely tilted, while Miriam whispered over her shoulder. He raised his eyebrows at me, smiling as he added, 'and thy wife', then looking to where Gershom and Eliezer waited coolly but with respect, 'and her two sons with her'.

We went, then, into my tent where, like a boy released from too much responsibility, I poured out all that the Lord had done in bringing us out of Egypt, all the travail we had borne on our journey, and all the safe keeping with which the Lord had encompassed us. I told him of my fears, my uncertainties, my weaknesses. I told him of the plagues and of the way I saw them. I told him, with pain, of Pharaoh and the blessing I had given. Even, I told him of the love – that God-directed love of neighbour

– which it had seemed possible, in that moment, to extend, without hypocrisy. There was our going out of Egypt, with Jethro's priestly face reflecting his joy as I spoke about the feast of the passing over which I had laid down as a memorial for ever. There was the resting on the seventh day. And finally there was the Sea of Reeds and what had happened there. My anguish. My complicity.

I even revealed to him that I saw the overthrow of the Egyptians not as the Lord's arbitrary disruption of his own laws, not as his hand, his breath, his will, reversing those tides which he himself had originally set in order, but as a vast, natural convulsion deep within the sea-bed, to which the Lord in his wisdom (holding, as he did, the entire creation within his comprehending glance) more subtly caused us to be guided: to be there, at that place, at that moment, on that day, when the waters would withdraw and our salvation would be accomplished. Equally a marvel, I told him, watching his considering gaze, yet with more of mystery than of magic. I saw him smile. But what the smile meant I did not know.

Eventually it was told, Jethro all the time conscious, as I was, that the great pillar of the Lord's presence brooded over our tent. And then, for the first time in many years, I felt a burden fall from my shoulders, as if a layer of corroding sores had been healed, leaving the skin whole beneath. The telling had been a purgation, from which I had emerged without sin. It was as if Jethro had lifted my load and taken it upon himself. His wise, bird-sharp eyes, smiling with acceptance and understanding, had, with a glance, dismissed my fears and discounted my weakness.

Outside, not long before the desert night came abruptly down, Jethro offered up thanksgiving to the people, as first one company, then another, left their tents and gathered near. Caleb and Joshua brought Gershom and Eliezer, both my sons less wooden now and even placing themselves timidly, yet proudly, beside me – an acceptance of me which I knew had come about not through my own presence but through the efforts of my two captains.

'Blessed be the Lord,' cried Jethro, raising his arms before the people, the wind lifting his white hair so that he looked, I thought, much as the early patriarchs must have looked, and with the same nobility and power, 'who hath delivered you out of the land of the Egyptians, and out of the hand of Pharaoh.'

The front ranks of the people were kneeling soberly before him.

'Now, I know,' he confessed, and it was as if his beautiful voice caressed their shoulders, 'that the Lord is greater than all gods.'

Then he took a burnt offering of thanksgiving, sacrificed to God, and after that Aaron came, and all the elders of Israel, to eat bread with my father-in-law, asking him questions and according him the respect given to one in rare authority.

Late into the next day it was Jethro who settled the matter of the waiting supplicants, gazing with exaggerated astonishment and a look of comic dismay which I well remembered.

'What is this thing that thou doest to the people?' He was laughing into his beard. 'Why sittest thou thyself alone, and all the people stand about thee from morning unto even?'

I replied stiffly, unsure of my dignity: 'Because the people come unto me to inquire of God.'

His eyebrows lifted high and, feeling as raw as my two young sons yet loving him for his ruthlessness, I hastened to add, though sounding still a little pompous: 'When they have a matter, they come to me; and I judge between a man and his neighbour, and I make them know the statutes of God, and his laws.'

But he shook his head, and the wry humour changed to a frown. 'The thing that thou doest is not good.' And he raised his hands, outlining my admittedly bare-boned form with a return of malicious wit. 'Thou shalt surely wear away, both thou, and the people that is with thee: for the thing is too heavy for thee; thou art not able to perform it thyself alone.'

So he counselled me, agreeing that I alone must teach the people the law of God and show them the way they must walk and the work they must do; but also, I must choose able men to be rulers and judges, so that, while the great matters were still to be brought to me, the smaller could be settled by others.

He studied me cautiously as he made this suggestion, and I could see that he was well aware of my pride.

'If thou shalt do this thing, then thou shalt be able to endure.' He chewed reflectively at his lower lip and, with an amused glance, added mockingly' 'And all thy people also.'

So I did what Jethro advised and chose capable men and made

them heads over the people, arranging it in an orderly fashion so that there were rulers over thousands, and beneath them rulers over hundreds and then over fifties and even over tens. When I had done this, I gathered my new rulers around me and told them, in simple terms, the precepts that should guide them in their decisions. 'Hear the causes between your brethren,' I charged them, 'and judge righteously between a man and his brother, and the stranger that is with him. Ye shall not respect persons in judgement; ye shall hear the small and the great alike; ye shall not be afraid of the face of man; for the judgement is God's: and the cause that is too hard for you ye shall bring unto me, and I shall hear it.'

Then, remembering my own solitary wanderings when I had received hospitality at strange tents, and remembering the name I had given my eldest son, I laid great stress upon their dealings with the outsider and the foreigner. 'And a stranger shalt thou not oppress,' I declared, 'for ye know the heart of a stranger, seeing ye were strangers in the land of Egypt.'

So I arranged it, and it was as if a load had again been lifted from me. But, in place of that load had come another, for I knew that Jethro would now depart from Horeb and return to his own land.

We made a feast for him, the night before his people took down their tents. We sat, our whole host, around the many fires that starred the valley with their points of light. We rejoiced in our companionship, even Zipporah relaxing her disdain when she found she was to be restored to her sisters.

I remembered, as I sat beside Jethro, close together with my sons and Aaron and Hur and Caleb and Joshua, how many times in the past – after I had wearied of Jethro's tents – I had sat in the wilderness beside my own small fire, listening to the silences of the desert and watching the dark shadows of mountains as they cut into the paler dark of the night sky. No music there – only the sound of the wind as it whistled down a gully. No dancing – only the rattle of dry leaves blowing across the sand. No singing – only the great solitude which yet had seemed as a song within me.

In the early dawn, I walked beyond the camp with Jethro, my

heart reluctant at losing him. Noting his increasing years, and knowing the journey that lay before my people, I understood that I should not see him again, this man in whom I had discovered my father. After the brief gift of his presence, I should stand even more alone.

So, at our parting, I knelt once more at his feet, my tears falling over his shoes, and when he raised me to his shoulder and clasped me in his arms, there was nothing that we needed to say to one another.

I watched his small caravan diminishing into the desert, shrinking at last to a faint mark upon the distant sand. Then he was gone.

——— XIV ———

The Presence

'Come up to me into the mount, and be there. . . .'

So, in another early dawn, I left my people and followed a narrow gully that led deep into the fastness of Horeb, rising steeply between shoulders of yellow rock. Below me a fuzz of dried bushes covered the stony plain. My people were out of sight. Only Joshua had stationed himself at a distance, patiently to await my safe return. Daybreak was still and windless, the rising sun brilliant. I made my way with the deliberation of long practice, climbing a parched watercourse where once a thin stream must have trickled. I carried nothing with me, neither food nor water, for I believed I must enter trustfully into the Lord's presence, unconcerned for the body's needs. Perhaps I was foolish. I know that Caleb, always the practical one, thought so. But Joshua had smiled, a reward for my folly.

Now, having carefully positioned himself so as to be visible to me, Joshua was standing in the open plain at the foot of the mountain, a tiny dot far down among the pale bushes. There was no sound, no movement save when a snake glided discreetly into a crevice, or when a loose pebble rolled down the track. Far overhead, mounting the topmost range of Horeb, I saw a speck that might have been an eagle. I smiled ruefully as I remembered my own soaring flight at the Sea of Reeds.

Strangely, I felt no heat, no discomfort, no hunger, no thirst. I moved without effort, seeing yet not seeing the stilled world, aware of a pause in the breathing of creation, conscious that the mountainside was being gathered quietly into the hand of God and held there, waiting.

I stopped quite suddenly, unwilling to go farther, as if I had been checked. When I looked back, I saw that a wall of rock had shut out all sight of the plain below, while in front of me the gully ended against a smooth escarpment. I stood in a bowl of yellow rock, so shaped that the light spilled over the rim, pouring into the place with a soft, luminous blur. Then, as I paused, obedient to what might come to me, I heard the voice of the Lord. It beat gently into me, pulsing within my blood. I knelt, aware of safe keeping, emptied of resistance. At the burning bush, I had been afraid. Now, I knelt in love, passionate to serve him.

'Thus shalt thou say to the house of Jacob, and tell the children of Israel. . . .' The Voice occupied me. 'Ye have seen what I did unto the Egyptians, and how I bore you on eagles' wings, and brought you unto myself. Now therefore, if ye will obey my voice indeed, and keep my covenant, then ye shall be a peculiar treasure unto me from among all peoples: for all the earth is mine.'

Borne on eagles' wings. To obey the Lord and keep his covenant. And to be to him a peculiar treasure. From among all peoples. . . .

I laid my forehead against the sand, seeing the desert's myriad grains as the myriad peoples of earth. Could this be possible for us? Could our unruly host be then the beginning of the Lord's enduring presence among those living grains? And if so, what would that mean for us? Not power, surely? Not triumph or glory. Rather, a terrible yet holy burden. One which we, unasked and unappreciated among those myriad grains, must carry. To be the witness, the messenger, the living fire. To be the vessel within which the Lord might be seen and recognised. He, walking the earth beside us and within us.

'And ye shall be unto me a kingdom of priests, and an holy nation.'

There it was. We were to become priests. A holy nation. But no one man alone. Not I, not Aaron, nor even those who would come after. Certainly not this fractious people immediately called to be the vessel, in this present time, of holiness. It would be all our people, out of all times, all lands, the good and the evil man bound up together. Once I had said, I cannot do this thing, I am not able. Now it was not just I who must accept this charge. And would they, any more than I, be able? Yet the Lord, even if he had set his conditions, had also made his promise.

I stored these thoughts into my being, hearing the Lord's dismissal: 'These are the words which thou shalt speak unto the children of Israel.'

So I rose to my feet, dazed with the inner beating of the Lord's voice, blinded by the bowl of light in which I stood. For a while there was silence in the place. Not the silence of barren rock in an empty land, but a silence that lay as a blessing upon each stone, each grain of sand, each small dry plant, each hidden, stealthy creature of the wilderness. For a long time I stood there, listening. Then I turned away and went down the side of the mountain, the tiny figure of Joshua, still resolutely unmoved, growing larger at each stride.

When I reached him, I found I could not speak. Not that my tongue was divided as of old, but simply that I was dumb. Indeed, I knew I had uttered no word in the Lord's presence, neither yea nor nay. So I stood before Joshua and pondered this. Yet it seemed that my presence had been sufficient. Recognised and accepted. Well, yes. He had dealt with me before. I stared blankly down at Joshua, surprised that he was kneeling before me. So I raised him up and we walked silently together, he remaining a hesitant step behind.

After I had returned to the encampment, my speech came back and I called together Aaron and my judges – those men whom I had placed in authority – and set before them the Lord's commands: to obey, and to keep the covenant. They also, I believe, understood the precarious nature of this task, yet they answered soberly: 'All that the Lord hath spoken we will do.'

This heartened me a little, and I gathered my people, after three days of purification, at the foot of the mountain, warning them that they should not go up into it, nor even touch its borders. For if they did, they would not abide the unleashed power of the Lord, and so would die.

It was a different mountain and a different day, and not one of my people would have either wished or dared to break the prohibition. A thick cloud lay over Horeb, and the mountain smoked and quaked. It seemed on fire with the Lord's undoubted indwelling, my people stunned by the thunder and blinded by the lightning. There was a sound like a trumpet coming out of the terrible darkness, and I thought – yet could not be sure – that the great figure of the malakh stood guard within the fire.

The people were afraid. Could it be otherwise? And when the Lord rebuked me that they had moved too close, I answered tartly. As indeed I was so often to do, pulled between my people and my God, both of them far from making common cause. The people, I told him, irritable in my apprehension as to how this strange meeting might turn out, would in no wise trespass on the mountain. Was it not set apart as a holy place? We knew this, I insisted, 'for thou didst charge us, set bounds about the mount and sanctify it'.

Then the Lord argued with me and in the end Aaron was permitted to toil up the unpropitious flank of Horeb – not very far, certainly, but even so it was an effort that taxed him sorely. But the Lord (may he forgive me) was right to set restrictions. Would it have been seemly for a great rabble of folk to storm Horeb? To invade the place of the Lord? Surely not, for how could they have borne his presence?

After this, the thunder and the trumpet died away, yet the smoke and the fire continued, the one a thick darkness, the other pure and soundless energy. It was then that the Lord spoke to his people and, turning, I saw that all lay prostrate and silent, stretched far out as a living skin over the yellow waste, motionless, even to the young children and the beasts.

'I am the Lord thy God which brought thee out of Egypt,' said the Lord, 'and out of the house of bondage.'

Some of them wept then, easily moved and remembering their slavery, so that when the Lord said sternly, 'Thou shalt have none other gods before me', a great cry of submission welled out of them and they spoke as Jacob our ancestor: Let us put away the strange gods that are among us, and purify ourselves, and change our garments.

The Lord listened – carefully, it seemed, and perhaps not altogether persuaded. 'Thou shalt not', he told them as they nodded their heads eagerly, and the floor of the desert appeared to ripple, 'make unto thee a graven image, the likeness of any form that is in heaven above, or that is in the earth beneath, or that is in the water under the earth.'

For a moment, I saw myself horned, but only as a passing flicker of recognition – the smaller manifestations to which I had become accustomed wiped out now in the greater manifestation of the Lord God of Israel.

'Thou shalt not bow down thyself unto them, nor serve them,' he continued, and they raised their faces which were marked with innocence. 'For I the Lord thy God am a jealous God, visiting the iniquity of the fathers upon the children, and upon the third and upon the fourth generation of them that hate me. . . .'

So they regarded their offspring with a certain anxiety, yet relieved, with a touch of complacency, as the Lord added softly: 'And showing mercy unto thousands of them that love me and keep my commandments.'

It was like an instrument which the Lord was playing, the people responding with smiles and tears as his words swept over them: 'Thou shalt not take the name of the Lord thy God in vain, for the Lord will not hold him guiltless that taketh his name in vain.'

This they did not understand, yet they must have perceived something of terror beneath the simple-seeming admonition, for they moved uneasily, crouching there in the hot sand against the unkind stones.

It was after this, to my joy, that the Lord confirmed the day of rest that I had established when we left the twelve springs of Elim.

'Observe the sabbath day,' he instructed them, 'to keep it holy, as the Lord thy God commanded thee. Six days shalt thou labour, and do all thy work: but the seventh day is a sabbath unto the Lord thy God: in it thou shalt not do any work, thou, nor thy son, nor thy daughter, nor thy manservant, nor thy maidservant, nor thine ox, nor thine ass, nor any of thy cattle, nor thy stranger that is within thy gates; that thy manservant and thy maidservant may rest as well as thou.

'And thou shalt remember that thou wast a servant in the land of Egypt, and the Lord thy God brought thee out thence by a mighty hand, and by a stretched out arm: therefore the Lord thy God commanded thee to keep the sabbath day.'

Now my people truly wept, and if they shed the easy tears of men and women so recently escaped from slavery, then those who wept could also understand the equity of these laws. There, before Mount Horeb, was gathered one community, their flocks included and also meriting rest. As for the stranger, had there been any such to come among them in that moment, surely they would have been caught to my people's hearts as being made in their own likeness?

By now, as the Lord passed from his worship to their dealings one with another, the people were squatting on the desert floor, their families close about them.

'Honour thy father and thy mother,' the Lord commanded, and they smiled, for that came easily to Israel, 'that thy days may be long, and that it may go well with thee upon the land which the Lord thy God giveth thee. Thou shalt do no murder. Neither adultery. Neither shalt thou steal. Thou shalt not bear false witness against thy neighbour. Neither shalt thou covet thy neighbour's wife. Nor shalt thou', said the Lord, 'desire his house, his field, or his manservant, or his maidservant, his ox, or his ass, or anything that is his.'

I thought of Amram, the father I had scarcely known. Of Jochebed, who had surrendered me – though that she could not help. Of the Egyptian princess, long since dead, who had fancied me for a while, only to find that I was not a plaything but a live and suffering human being, compounded of anger and loyalty and – yes – gratitude, but reserving my soul for the God of Israel and my heart for his people.

The pull of that early discord ran ever through me, as active now as when I had been a stripling. But now I recognised my plight and could make some show of mastering it. I thought then of Jethro, working his way towards that distant land of his. He at least had given me the birthright of love.

The Voice fell silent, and I shook back into myself. The mountain smoked more furiously, the thunder stirred again out of the darkness, and the fire poured over the rocks in rivers of light. Those who were nearer removed themselves somewhat hastily, standing irresolute while the elders and judges came to meet me. 'Behold,' they said, and some looked embarrassed, as if disliking what had to be said, 'the Lord our God hath showed us his glory and his greatness, and we have heard his voice out of the midst of the fire: we have seen this day that God doth speak with man, and he liveth.'

The words came agreeably, yet there was fear also and the men were shifty-eyed. I despaired, because they were the chosen leaders upon whose shoulders rested wisdom and courage and good understanding. Seeing my mistrust, they began to bluster.

'Now therefore,' they went on, trying not to see the flames and flinching from the thunder, 'why should we die? For this great fire will consume us: if we hear the voice of the Lord our God any more, we shall die.'

'For who is there of all flesh,' interrupted one who had been silent, 'that hath heard the voice of the living God speaking out of the midst of the fire, as we have, and lived?'

They hustled me, not fawning, but eager to coerce. 'Go thou near,' they urged, 'and hear all that the Lord our God shall say. And speak thou unto us all that the Lord our God shall speak unto thee; and we will hear it, and do it.'

I swung away from them, angered and sick at heart because they were cowards, and it seemed to me as if I could hear the Lord's sorrowing: 'Oh, that there were such an heart in them, that they would fear me, and keep all my commandments always, that it might be well with them, and with their children for ever! Go say to them, Return ye to your tents.'

And as I moved to do the Lord's bidding, his voice followed me: 'But as for thee, stand thou here by me, and I shall speak unto thee all the commandments, and the statutes, and the judgements, which thou shalt teach them, that they may do them in the land which I give them to possess it.'

But even as I began to speak, the heads of the different tribes entreated me. 'Speak thou with us,' they cried in panic, 'and we shall hear. But let not God speak with us, lest we die.'

I tried to tell them they should not fear the voice of the Lord but rather fear the breaking of his commandments. But they would not listen and speedily backed away, my brother Aaron being one of them. So I left them and returned to the mountain, drawing near to the fire and the smoke where the Lord awaited me.

Yet had I not also rejected the Lord when first he called me? Was it then so light a matter, to have speech with the living God? And were my people, even the ablest of them, not understandably a little dubious at remaining in his presence? Truly, there was darkness as well as light, and fire as well as honey. And truly it would be easy to incur his wrath. These were my thoughts as I went up into the mountain, wondering if I myself would live were I to trespass across the border of his power, or touch the prohibited places of Horeb.

Stubbornly I climbed until the fringes of cloud enveloped me and nothing more could be seen of the desert or of my people. Perhaps, I comforted myself, the Lord had need of me. To interpret his will. Would not that be a safeguard?

XV

None Other Gods

No yellow bowl of light. Only the cloud, and the lightning playing about my shoulders. Only the rock on which I sat, and the patch of ground beneath my feet where, occasionally, I knelt. No time. Only the enormous monologue of the Lord.

Afterwards, it was all to be written down – a lasting testimony for my people. Yet in all the forty years of our wanderings, I forgot no word of it. The letters were imprinted upon my bones; they rested in the sockets of my eyes; they flowed behind my tongue and in the river of my blood.

The Lord spoke to me of justice and mercy; of hate and love; of violence and compassion; life and death. The justice was unmitigated, the mercy contingent. The hate was not to be borne; the love was entire. The violence and compassion were knit together in our redemption. The life was obedience, and death the comforting of his hand.

I listened to his words, yet made no effort to remember them. Perhaps I knew that effort was not required, that I was to be merely the living book from which his commandments would be transcribed on to more durable material. Yet, as I waited in his presence, I knew also that my mind was busy with the meaning of everything he told me, my stubborn, awkward, tenacious spirit ever disputing the words till they fitted my own pattern.

And certainly it was not an easy message. It seemed that the pastures we would inherit were to be earned by our stumbling, punished feet and inevitably to be watered with the tears of our transgressions. Justice, I could see, was to be harsh. Yet not for nothing had I travelled the wilderness in my youth, shuddering from reports of demon worship and that retributive torture of body and spirit which passed for judgement. The justice of the Lord was of a different kind. 'Life for life,' he declared, 'eye for eye, tooth for tooth, hand for hand, foot for foot, burning for burning, wound for wound, stripe for stripe.'

But not more. Not several lives for one life. Not two eyes for one. Not two hands or many stripes. No longer, then, a tormented death extravagantly desecrating the human body, but a necessary stage on the way to a more sober appraisal of the human situation. Indeed, there was even a wisdom incomprehensible in our day: that the man who had injured another 'shall pay for the loss of his time, and shall cause him to be thoroughly healed'. An alien concept, but one which I welcomed.

Unaware of cold or heat, hunger or thirst, my heart was glad of these decisions of the Lord. Yet at times I trembled and rebelled, for I am not a man of war and would have avoided its cruelty. That this would not be allowed me, I already understood, so I listened bleakly to the Lord's inexorable command. 'Behold,' he said to me, 'I send an angel before thee, to keep thee by the way, and to bring thee into the place which I have prepared. Take ye heed of him, and hearken unto his voice; provoke him not: for he will not pardon your transgression; for my name is in him. But if thou shalt indeed hearken unto his voice, and do all that I speak, then I will be an enemy unto thine enemies, and an adversary unto thine adversaries. For mine angel shall go before thee, and bring thee in unto the Amorite, and the Hittite, and the Perizzite, and the Canaanite, the Hivite, and the Jebusite. . . .'

The Lord paused and I knew great fear. '. . . and I will cut them off,' he finished coldly.

Why? I cried to him then, in passionate revolt. They had not harmed us. But I knew the answer, for the tribes were soaked in blood. I recalled the tales I had heard: sacrificing their own kind, even – or preferably – the new-born children offered to their terrible bits of stone.

'Thou shalt not bow down to their gods,' retorted the Lord angrily, so that I fell to the ground as if lightning had struck me, 'nor serve them, nor do after their works: but thou shalt utterly overthrow them, and break in pieces their pillars.'

Then he added, perhaps to quell my rebellion, for I would have wished, susceptible and over-credulous as I am, that they too might have been saved: 'And ye shall serve the Lord your God, and he shall bless thy bread and thy water,' adding, as if in afterthought, 'and I will take sickness away from the midst of thee.'

I wondered, then, if he meant the sickness of our inconstant minds which so easily centred on the many rather than the one. 'I am the Lord thy God, I am the Lord thy God,' he told me over and over again, the inescapable, haunting message of his singularity. I saw, as I knelt before him, how immense was the way in which he would lead us. 'Ye shall not make other gods with me,' he had said. 'Gods of silver, or gods of gold, ye shall not make unto you.' And there were his words spoken already to my people: 'I am the Lord thy God . . . thou shalt have none other gods before me.'

In the midst of the pale, insubstantial cloud and with all humankind blotted out below me, I knew what this would mean. He would remove my people from the infection of corruption. He would pluck them from the overlapping, unreliable world of dark, conflicting magic. From now on there were to be no impertinent small gods. We were to fix our eyes only upon the One Lord God, Creator of the universe.

'And in all things that I have said unto you' – the Voice echoed my thought – 'take ye heed: and make no mention of the name of other gods, neither let it be heard out of thy mouth.'

The images around which men and women danced were but illusion; the Lord God was never to be found in the carved representations of power. He dwelt apart, in his own place which was not our place, and we could not conjure him by compulsive rites. But also – and here was his ambiguous mercy – he would dwell with us and his voice would speak our tongue. So, in the bringing about of all this, there was to be triumph and greatness for us, though clearly much suffering. There would be meekness and ferocity. And there would be death and death and death. Yet, over it all, we would be sheltered within the Lord's compassion, for we had been chosen. Would not a man, then, gladly give his life? The escape from Egypt now seemed an irrelevance, a trivial start on this long journey out of violence into love.

Already I was rehearsing in my mind the words I would speak to my people. 'The Lord did not set his love upon you,' I would tell them, 'nor choose you, because ye were more in number than any people, for ye were the fewest of all peoples. But because the Lord loveth you and because he would keep the oath which he swore unto your fathers, hath the Lord brought you out with a mighty hand.'

I knelt there weeping, and the words poured through me.

'And he will love thee, and bless thee, and multiply thee; he will also bless the fruit of thy body and the fruit of thy ground, thy corn and thy wine and thine oil, the increase of thy kine and the young of thy flock, in the land which he swore unto thy fathers to give thee.'

Still kneeling, still weeping, I raised my voice, as if my people, far below, might prick up their ears and attend. 'Hear, O Israel,' I cried aloud, 'the Lord our God is one Lord.'

All this I was to tell my people – not only the great things of the Lord, but the smaller things. For there were also those proper dealings of one man with another, whether the good or the evil man, in every ordered detail of our daily life. These, I would gradually instil. And when the Lord described our feast days and how we were to offer him the first fruits of our labour, I rejoiced then that he was turning our sacrifices to a more agreeable offering than hitherto. For the animals that we killed – not viciously to honour a stick or stone but often casually and then eaten with little discrimination, and sometimes fired to conciliate what may have seemed a bored and distant God – must now be offered in due ceremony and strictly defined order. There would still be blood upon the altar, but not, as with surrounding tribes, the blood of men or women or children. It would be the blood of beasts, yes, but accorded a clean death, then offered first for the Lord's blessing. Only after that sober performance might we ourselves satisfy our hunger.

And the blood, though we would shed it, belonged entirely to the Lord, the seat of life – indeed life itself and therefore holy, a channel of atonement, his life within the life offered – and never to be consumed by us unworthy ones.

It is true: I wrestled obstinately with myself, always identifying with the beasts we needed to kill (but did we eat sand?). Life, I felt, is composed of much beauty, and of death, yet even death can be compassionate.

I thought I could foresee a ritual where, in contrition over his own shortcomings, the owner of the beast would place his hand upon its waiting head to confess his sin. Thus, sacrifice would no longer remain a coercion, the placating of a jealous god, as with the outer tribes, but an acknowledgement that we are all, man and beast, in relationship. Our offering would be lifted up from butchery to the foreshadowing of our holy meal.

As I contemplated this, I saw a little further, towards that offering which would take our sin into its own innocence. I saw the horned goat being driven out to bear our iniquity; we, washed of guilt at the price of its submission. I shivered, for this was not a thought I wished to pursue. So I attended to the Lord as he turned to less disturbing if equally perplexing matters. 'And I will set thy border,' he told me, 'from the Reed Sea even unto the sea of the Philistines, and from the wilderness unto the river; for I will deliver the inhabitants of the land into your hands; and thou shalt drive them out before thee.'

My hands? To drive them out? I shrank from any such idea. No, rather my people's hands. I must be clean. But was I not the hands of my people? Being the Lord's messenger would also mean overcoming the demon worshippers; not to be done, I knew, with fair words but with blood. This, too, I had to prepare myself for. Unwilling.

With the Lord's words secure within me, I went down the mountain and set up an altar, resting it on twelve pillars, one for each of the tribes of Israel. The young men laid burnt offerings, and peace offerings of oxen sacrificed to the Lord. And I took part in sprinkling the blood which belonged not to us but to the giver of life.

It was while I stood there, confused amid the ritual clamour yet seeing also a new pattern emerging in which my people modified their acts before the Lord, that I noticed a gaunt, wild figure standing on the edge of the crowd. He was tall – far taller than I, who am not of great stature – with a lean face and hanging hair. His garments tossed in an unfelt wind, rippling as they flattened against his long, muscular thighs. His hands were uplifted, bony fingers curled in repudiation. His eyes were hollow pits, holding fire. It was the face of one stricken and afflicted. I heard his voice, but only I appeared to be aware of his presence.

'Wherewith shall I come before the Lord, and bow myself before the high God?' he cried in anguish. 'Shall I come before him with burnt offerings, with calves of a year old? Will the Lord be pleased with thousands of rams, or with ten thousand rivers of oil?'

The voice was enraged and bitter and I stood aghast, so that my people walked carefully around me, unheeding of his great untidy figure. And when I raised frightened eyes and looked at him, I knew he saw me clearly, fastening his angry gaze upon me from across the centuries. 'What doth the Lord require of thee,' he demanded, hands now open and extended, as if in homage. (Homage? How could that be? For surely he must be some distant prophet? Far greater than I and more certain of his purposes?) 'What doth the Lord require of thee,' he asked again, more gently, 'but to do justly, and to love mercy, and to walk humbly with thy God?'

Then he was gone. I reached after him, but at length turned back to the altar which he seemed so fiercely to deny. Yet I was now at peace with what we had to do. In his great wisdom, the Lord would lead us mildly if inexorably, not in such haste that my people stumbled, but bringing our ignorance, in the end, to a better usage. Perhaps this man also had trouble, in that time of his so far ahead of mine, but I knew, here in this my own moment, that both he and I would be vindicated and that the burning sacrifices would eventually become the infinitely more difficult offering of ourselves: that we might indeed do justly, loving mercy and walking humbly with our God.

In the place of bullocks would come the sanctification I had witnessed at that distant table, as the woman of the house kindled the Sabbath light. Using the tongue of God and his angels, she would call down loving kindness upon my people. And the things which the Lord had made holy, those new materials of our regeneration, would be shared. The wine which the Lord our God had created would gladden us. The bread which the Lord our God had brought forth from the earth would strengthen our hearts, even though it might frequently become also the broken bread of our adversity.

XVI

The Return from the Mountain

On the following day, as I had been bidden, I prevailed upon some of my people to come with me into the presence of the Lord. Aaron agreed reluctantly, well knowing that, if any were to go, he must be among them. Two of his four sons, Nadab and Abihu, came also, they being eager and ashamed of earlier hesitation. I was glad of them, yet uncertain in my mind, for it seemed to me – though without just cause – that they, like their father, were not entirely reliable. Rather, had it been the younger Eleazar who might, with encouragement, show himself made of better stuff.

My own two sons I did not take, for I considered them unready and even indifferent. Too hasty a judgement – and surely, a condemnation? But always I found myself ill at ease with them, increasingly unable to surmount the rising wall of their combined hostility. Jethro's care had not outweighed Zipporah's influence, and in the end I did not win them to me. This, I knew, was largely because of my blundering, my clumsiness. Even because of those abrupt retreats of mine, which must have suggested lack of interest. I knew those moments well, when, out of habit, I removed myself into some other layer of existence and became unapproachable. I recognised, too, my own impatience, unwilling to give them time. Yet time itself was not the ground of our difficulties, and the fault lay with me. Though must one man only, I asked myself, bear a fault? I found no answer, knowing only that on the rare occasions we were together I met their sullen rebuff, as I did with Zipporah. And maybe they had inherited, along with her resentments, something of my own obstinate reticence. Hardly an easy mixture.

So I left them behind, setting off with Aaron and his sons and seventy of the elders of Israel, most of them embarrassed at this excursion and exceedingly doubtful. They made a deal of trouble, climbing the short way into Horeb, so that I was all the more wrathful when, suddenly enraptured, they fell to their knees, shouting excitedly and throwing up their arms, though first eyeing each other askance and only then assiduously copying the one in front. It seemed they beheld a vision.

I stared up the bare track along the watercourse, now almost blotted out by the Lord's descending cloud. That the Lord himself was there, I did not doubt. But it appeared now that my people knew even better than I and, marvelling, could see him distinctly. He was there, they cried, their ecstasy spreading like a fever, standing before them in all his glory. Beneath his feet, they assured me in a babble of simple wonder, stretched a pavement of sapphire, transparent as heaven itself.

And still I gazed bluntly at the uncompromising rock, seeing no sapphire floor but only the thickening veils of cloud, out of which leapt small, angry tongues of flame. Perversely, and remembering my own meetings with the Lord, I found the vision unlikely. No jewelled platform half-way up the rocky slope of Horeb. How could that be? Some of the elders, I reasoned, had merely seen the things they conjectured would be there. Others, as Aaron – who was not given to a fervent imagination – were determined not to be outseen. So they wailed with exultation and beat their breasts, even leaping to their feet and twirling round in frenzied enthusiasm. I looked for Joshua, but could not see his face, for he was bent over, covering his eyes from the clownish spectacle. At length, exhausted by so much gratification, and with the vision perhaps a little spent, they reclined among the rocks, eating and drinking at their ease, as if no particular respect need be paid even to the Lord God of Israel whom they claimed to have met face to face.

But the presence of the Lord was no longer among us, his hands withdrawn from blessing.

Seeing all this, I despaired. Like mischievous, small children they had been caught for a brief moment in the pleasant fantasy of a marvel, distracted by its charm. The matters that I had already made known to them (hearing over again their solemn promises that 'all the words which the Lord hath spoken shall we do') had washed over their heads in a froth of insignificance, and now they envisaged the Lord God of Israel, the sovereign Creator of the universe, as some spell-conjured figure adequate to their own frivolous conceit.

Yet even as I belittled them, the bile rising in my mouth, I struggled – as I ever would – to excuse their foolishness. The stuff of greatness was not easily to be found in a people condemned to slavery and only now, after four hundred years, escaped into a freedom which must seem to them improbable and certainly open to suspicion. Maybe, too, there had been jealousy – I in conversation with the Lord and they resentful of my privilege – so that, this time, they intended seeing more than I could claim to see. Also – and this gave me pause – I foresaw a time, not yet come, when I myself, impertinently stretching out to touch reality, would beg the Lord to show himself to me. In that hour, he would refuse.

'I shall make all my goodness pass before thee,' he would say, 'and shall proclaim the name of the Lord before thee; and I shall be gracious to whom I shall be gracious, and shall show mercy on whom I shall show mercy.' But, he would add, and his voice would sound both terrible and grieved: 'Thou canst not see my face: for man shall not see me and live.'

And I would beseech him until, in my foolishness, I would hide within a cleft of the rock, covered by his hand. Then to behold, or so I would imagine, the granted dispensation of his departing form. Yet, could this be? Was it not more likely that I, to appease the grasping child within myself, would have been mistaken? But he had said: 'I shall take away my hand, and thou shalt see my back: but my face shall not be seen.' Even so, I would not be sure.

So, with great distaste and scarcely controlled contempt, yet also torn by pity for their deficiencies and disgust at my readiness to condemn, I left them. But first I ordered the elders to the foot of the mountain, there to await my return, and gave to Aaron and Hur the judgement of any cause which the people might bring during my absence.

Then I went up into Horeb, accompanied for part of the way by Joshua, aware of his distress yet aware also that I was empty and could not help him. When I left him at a turn in the path, he offered me such a look of compassionate discernment, as if he were the elder and I but a child, that I took him by the shoulder and blessed him, my heart lifting with the knowledge of his imperturbable steadfastness.

As once again I climbed slowly up the watercourse, I took myself bitterly to task for my lack of charity. What harm was done, I argued, if they relaxed a little in the company of their God? What harm in breaking bread in his presence? Must everything always be so solemn? And, since the Lord himself was busy at arranging their future relationships one with another, might it not be thought that he was able to abide their absurdity?

I saw myself as hypocritical and without sympathy – diminished, because I offered no response to their inoffensive bids for sensation, stiff and unbending in my pride. Had I perhaps grown too austere under the pressure of this task, no longer to be seen as the tranquil bearer of the Lord's spirit, but dimmed now and encrusted with all the perplexities of managing this great host of people? For indeed I had changed. This I recognised. Even in the few months since we had left Egypt I had become – yes – more prosaic, growing irascible under the ceaseless turmoil of my people's plaints and the rumble of their discontent.

As I savoured this fact, halted in the curve of a rising wall of rock, I sensed a flickering foreknowledge of my own haunted face, closer now than in the shadowed future I sometimes apprehended, and bearing the marks of indecision and defeat. I thought the time was nearly with me when I should inhabit that face, dropping from my uplifted arms some burden I could no longer sustain. The face told me everything about myself. It was my close companion, that other image of the self I should prefer to display.

Now, as I could see, it hardly exhibited that chosen messenger who walked in rapture at the Lord's command. The rapture had hardened, lying in a tight knot within me. Feeding me still, but not for all to see, not easily to be witnessed. I thought of Jethro and wished him near, but knowing that I alone must carry this burden. I remembered the burning bush, and how it had been dry when the glory had left it. It is not easy always to be fresh and green.

So I came contrite into the Lord's presence, muddled as I ever seemed to be by my own contradictions. And perhaps he tempered his teaching on this day in order to repair my lumpish spirit, talking not of the complexities of behaviour, or of punishment, or of the strictness of the law, but telling me about the tent of meeting we were to construct in his honour, within which his presence would be known and where his testimony was to be treasured and where he would be worshipped.

The structure was shadowed forth even to the last particularity: from the cups of the branched golden candlestick, each shaped into almond blossom, to the sockets of silver, binding together the acacia-wood boards of the tabernacle; from the ten great woven curtains of blue and purple and scarlet which would surround the holy place, to the mercy seat of pure gold; from the two cherubim, spreading out their golden wings, to the golden ark which would contain the Lord's testimony. There would be the veil, which was to conceal the ark and which was also of blue and purple and scarlet. There would be the incense altar and the table which was to bear the vessels, both overlaid with gold. There would be the seven lamps, and the pillars of gold and the pillars of silver. And for the outer covering, there would be the curtains of goats' hair and the covering of red-dyed rams' skins bearing sealskins above.

Afterwards I marvelled at the telling of it. Did the Lord speak with me in my own speech, precisely enunciating the exact structure in all its detailed complexity? Or did he, rather, create it whole within me, established in such visual clarity that I was able to distinguish each thread of wool, each cunning silver link, each fine disposition of its many wonders? I could not be sure. Only , that my inner sight received it complete, while the words seemed to crystallise it within me. My words? Or the Lord's? That I did not know. In some mysterious fashion all this intricate knowledge was grafted on to me and in my imagination I saw the place where we would meet our God, a shining tent which would house his presence, a sanctuary of such beauty, such colour and such dignity that I could scarcely believe it possible in this barren wilderness of sand. Yet it burst into flower within my vision, and so strong was its impress, so vivid its portrayal in the sight of my mind, that I could almost forgive my people their sapphire pavement.

'And there', said the Lord, as the smoke and the tongues of fire vanished and a clear light flowed once more over the lip of my yellow bowl of rock, 'I shall meet with the children of Israel: and the tent shall be sanctified to my glory. And I shall sanctify the tent of meeting, and the altar: Aaron also and his sons shall I sanctify, to minister to me in the priest's office. And I shall dwell among the children of Israel, and be their God.'

Here I gave thanks, my foolish tears trickling into my beard. At last there would be a task for Aaron – some real power, that he might be a little satisfied, might parade himself before the people yet be obedient to the Lord's purposes.

'And bring thou near unto thee Aaron thy brother . . .' – this was reproof, and I knew then that I had indeed set myself apart – '. . . and his sons with him, from among the children of Israel, that he may minister unto me in the priest's office, even Aaron, Nadab and Abihu, Eleazar and Ithamar, Aaron's sons.'

I nodded confidently. A burden had been lifted.

'And thou shalt make holy garments for Aaron thy brother, for glory and for beauty,' he told me.

A most astonishing beauty: for upon the skirts of his blue garment would be embroidered pomegranates of blue and purple and scarlet, with little bells of gold hanging between the pomegranates. There would be a coat in chequerwork of fine linen. There was to be an upper garment of blue and purple and scarlet wool, threaded through with gold, and a breastplate bearing precious stones which would signify the twelve tribes of Israel. All this and more would there be of beauty and glory. And then the Lord said a strange thing, which I did not understand. 'And Aaron', he told me, 'shall bear the iniquity of the holy things.'

This seemed to me a heavy matter: that the priest who bore the names of the people of Israel on his jewelled breastplate should also bear their judgement. I quailed from such a destiny and, when the Lord described the altar at which Aaron was to serve, it seemed that this too would be encompassed with great peril. Aaron, I was told, must make atonement upon the altar for the people's sins, and this was to be done once in every year. He would, it is true, be sanctified to the task, anointed as the High Priest of Israel, yet it seemed to me that such a privilege carried great penalty and that the priest and his sons would need to tread a knife-edge of holiness.

When the Lord had finished speaking to me, I came back into myself. The time of the Lord, which had caught me into a single breath of his eternity, now surrendered me to the time, the dreadful time, of this passing world. I became aware of the mountain, but no longer of the light-filled bowl. Only darkening cloud and the fire tremulous.

In silence I received from him the two stone tablets of his testimony, written with his finger. These I had known would be given me, and I acknowledged them from that other time, once experienced. Now I held them in my hands.

So I went down the mountain, bearing them. But not in ecstasy. Perhaps never again in ecstasy. For, in the end, there had been the unexpected tumult of his wrath. So that now I held a death within me, many deaths, and I walked in fear, engulfed by the Lord's bitter fury.

When I reached the place where my people were, and when I saw, and when I looked about me, I knew that now indeed had my face become that other face I should have wished to repudiate: a shadowed face, untenanted, showing forth emptiness, and dispossessed.

Encaged within that other self, I raised the tablets above my head. Then, opening my stiff, cramped fingers, I let them drop. They fell heavily, rumbling down a small ravine, splitting upon a rock and breaking into small, clattering pieces which bounced into the gully far below my feet.

So I destroyed them.

And suddenly, when it was done, the face I now inhabited – the face of the victim – exploded into fragments, even as the tablets had done, and bits of me burst apart and flew terribly in all directions, so that the thunder and lightning of the Lord raged through me.

My anger. For my people had betrayed their God.

XVII

The Golden Calf

'There is a noise of war in the camp.'

This had been uttered by Joshua, slowly and without emotion, as if thoughtfully breaking some terrible rumour. And, before that, as I left the mountain, the Lord himself had spoken: 'Go, get thee down: for thy people, which thou broughtest up out of the land of Egypt, have corrupted themselves.'

No longer, then, a people belonging to the Lord, but mine, all mine. 'Thy' people, he had said dismissively, thrusting them upon me. I was to be responsible, since I alone had brought them here, the Lord having washed his hands of them. 'A stiff-necked people . . .' – the Voice bitter and unforgiving – '. . . quickly turned aside out of the way I commanded them.'

I had knelt humbly, but thinking that such inconstancy might perhaps have been expected, and hearing the Lord's gathering wrath with anxiety, dismayed at his accusations. An idol, he had said. And sacrifice. The worship of a golden calf. . . .

'These be thy gods, O Israel,' he raged, 'which brought thee up out of the land of Egypt.'

But this I could not believe, knowing them to be foolish in small things, yet judging them trustworthy in great.

The thunder had grown louder and the Lord's voice plunged in rods of lightning, so that I shrivelled before his anger. The words whirled over me in a rising spiral of storm: '. . . that I may destroy them, and blot out their name from under heaven. . . . That my wrath may wax hot against them, so that I may consume them. . . .'

Appalled by his ferocity, doubting him in my confusion, none the less I challenged him. 'Lord,' I had begged in my distress, 'why dost thy wrath wax hot against thy people?' Yes, 'thy' people. I made it plain. 'Which thou hast brought forth out of the land of Egypt with great power and with a mighty hand?' That, too, made plain. Defying him with my 'thou'. Not I but the Lord bringing them forth. His responsibility. Not mine. Not.

Why, I had asked myself, this irrational fury? To consume them? From the face of the earth? I expostulated with him, outraged by what seemed to be his capricious perversity. Then, still upon my knees: 'Turn from thy fierce wrath, and repent of this evil against thy people,' I had admonished. How could I dare?

Yet assuredly I could not understand it. One moment pouring out the riches of his testimony, the next determined to destroy.

'Remember Abraham, Isaac and Israel, thy servants,' I had the temerity to recommend, 'to whom thou swearest by thine own self, and saidst unto them, I shall multiply your seed as the stars of heaven. . . .'

And it seemed as if the Lord repented a little of his implacable rage. But only a little.

So I had turned and had gone down from the mountain, bearing the tablets and meeting a haggard Joshua on the way.

War in the camp, Joshua had said, and I had known he was preparing me for catastrophe. Afterwards I asked myself why I had docilely accepted his quiet statements while daring to discredit the Lord's omniscience. Perhaps the violent change of mood had been too much for me. Perhaps I had always been afraid that the whole precarious venture might come to nothing.

'It is not the voice of those who shout for mastery,' Joshua had continued, licking his lips and avoiding my eyes, 'neither is it the voice of those who cry for being overcome.' Joshua hesitated, again turning upon me that look of compassionate experience. 'But the voice of those who sing do I hear.' And indeed I too could now distinguish the sounds of a wild chanting.

Then kneeling before me, he had told me all that the people were doing: how, while I had been upon Horeb within that time which was outside time, the people had grown weary of my delay, and had gathered round Aaron in protest. They had said, explained Joshua, now flinching from my look: 'Up, make us gods, which shall go before us: for as for this Moses . . .' – his face had crumpled – '. . . the man that brought us up out of the land of Egypt, we know not what has become of him.'

And Aaron? I had asked, my tongue following its almost forgotten habit and sticking in my throat.

'And Aaron said unto them . . .' – here Joshua had glanced this way and that, unwilling to play the informant – 'Break off the golden rings, which are in the ears of your wives, of your sons, and of your daughters, and bring them unto me.'

And?

Joshua had hidden his eyes from me, saying in a low voice: 'He received it at their hand, and fashioned it with a graving tool, and made it a molten calf: and they said . . . and they said. . . .'

Then he spoke the words with which the Lord had already taunted me: 'These be thy gods, O Israel.'

I had been stricken to silence, listening as if palsied and blind while Joshua told me how Aaron had built an altar and proclaimed a feast and that they had risen up early and offered burnt sacrifice to the golden calf and that they had danced around it and worshipped it. . . . They had worshipped it. . . . But here I had been shaking like a reed in a strong wind, still clasping the tablets in my robe, and still in this quiet and awful dream where I strove to thrust from me what surely could not be.

So we had come down to the camp and I had seen the golden calf and the altar and the dancing; I now fully in possession of that haunted victim face I knew so well. It was then, in my anger, that I had cast the tablets from me.

Had I but contained the power of the Lord, I should in that moment have struck them down, even as the Lord God of Israel had threatened. But lacking it, I swept in a fury through the trembling throng of dancers, seizing the calf they had made, wresting it out of the smoke and the smell of burning flesh, and grinding it to powder. Then, possessed still by a terrible vengeance, I mixed the gold dust with water and forced the seventy elders, and Aaron and his sons, to drink it. They grovelled before me, uncertain, I now believe, as to whether I could be their meek, accustomed prophet, or whether my fury-swollen body housed the Lord himself in all his wrath.

Then I had Aaron brought before me, even while the smoke of sacrifice still curled about the tents and the smell sickened upon the dead air. I spoke to him out of a cold passion, and my tongue obeyed me, so that my words struck him like blows.

'What did this people unto thee, that thou hast brought a great sin upon them?'

He eyed me shiftily, so that I began to scent a deeper prompting than his weakness.

'Let not the anger of my lord wax hot.' His voice was smooth but his lips were shaking, while his ringed hand tried to paw me with fellowship. I thrust him off. Then, with a lift of his shoulder and a grimace of complicity, he threw out his arm, gesturing contemptuously at the terrified crowds. 'Thou knowest the people . . .' – attempting now an easy disdain – '. . . that they are set on evil.'

I looked around me to where they were cowering; even Miriam with her timbrel slipped hastily inside her tent.

'They said to me,' continued Aaron, coughing a little and wiping his forehead: 'Make us gods, which shall go before us: for . . .' – and here a spark of malice flickered at the back of his eyes as he carefully repeated what Joshua had told me – '. . . as for this Moses, the man that brought us up out of the land of Egypt, we know not what is become of him.'

Here, Aaron swung his robe about him, making it an evidence of authority, and telling me as it were but a trifle: 'And I said to them, Whosoever hath any gold, let them break it off: so they gave it me: and I cast it into the fire and there came out this calf.' Here he spat uncomfortably, the dust he had so reluctantly swallowed appearing to stick in his throat.

I stood in silence, watching Aaron, watching the huddled people – they broken loose into an orgy of idol worship and now dishevelled and filthy and stained. I questioned Aaron's hidden look. There was purpose in what he had done, a design to lead to his own enlargement, but directed at the world which lay outside our own people. That much was clear. What was it he had done? I asked myself, still regarding him with repugnance, he – even he – not daring to remove himself. And looking around me at the disarray, at the blood-encrusted faces, the kicked-up dust, the piles of dirt, the reeking plumes of smoke, seeing the grease and the charred altar, and the portions of rotting carcases, I knew what it was.

He had been busy about the task of diminishing my people: of discrediting them, of bringing them into contempt. And I saw in a great gust of revelation that he had let them loose for derision among their enemies. The desert is a lonely place and the tribes live a secret life and hidden. But word travels fast, and even now we would be a laughing-stock: this holy people, this peculiar treasure (and here I shook, but I must not, no, I must not . . .), this kingdom of priests, borne on eagles' wings to keep – yes, to keep the covenant. . . . How they had fallen, it would be said, and we would be held in scorn.

But why? What could have been Aaron's purpose? I stared at him while he shifted uneasily, alarmed by something in my look. The answer, of course, was power; the bid for a wider empire than this bedraggled host of vacillating, feckless people. A compact with our enemies.

Curiously, my spirit lightened, for I realised that if only I could placate the anger of the Lord, there might still be redemption for us. And the power that Aaron was slyly looking for, striving after it through the degradation of his own people, might become power of a different kind, harnessed to the Lord's purposes and cleansing both him and the people.

I sighed. At which Aaron visibly relaxed. Perhaps he was not entirely evil. Perhaps he was that more dreary problem, a weak and hungry man.

First there must be expiation. I recognised it with the full authority of the Lord's unappeased anger beating within me. But it was my own anger also, grown cold and relentless, a new, unnerving, bitter resolution. It lurked, I knew, behind my bleak, mistrusting eyes. It was there, open for all to see, in my mouth's unfamiliar jutting of disgust. My people must be purged, and in my strange, new-found, savage resolve I saw that they themselves would respond only to an adequate retribution.

So I stood back a little, then mounted a small platform brought by Caleb and Joshua.

'Whoso is on the Lord's side,' I told the people – a new voice, a new judge, unleashed now from former meekness – 'let him come unto me.'

There was a long silence, a shifting in the crowds, much hesitation and even a wave of withdrawal, as if they would rather their golden calf than the Lord God of Israel with his harsh edicts. Then, one by one, bringing others with them, furtive and ashamed, all the sons of Levi gathered themselves about me: the tribe of Aaron my brother, of Miriam my sister – my own tribe, my own blood brothers. I could have wept with thankfulness. But I did not. Only a deep cold seized my heart and I told the sons of Levi to take their swords upon their thighs and to go from gate to gate throughout the camp, and to kill all those – the intractable and unrepentant – who had incited the people; pulling each leader from his tent and, where they found him obdurate, taking his life despite all tears.

And I looked at Aaron, now standing with me among his own family, and watched his face, seeing the sweat rolling into his beard. Then I crooked my finger and he came to me like a dog, obedient, and I told him that he should not go with the Levites, or any of his four sons, and I told him then what might come out of this day. Shaking, he fell down before me, and he wept. In all my days I had not seen Aaron weep.

Afterwards, with the slaughter done and the people subdued, I told them how they had sinned a great sin, and to wash themselves, purifying their garments so that, together, we might make fresh vows of consecration. When this, too, was done, I, still clad within the iron of my resolution, and shutting my ears to the wailing over the many dead, told them I would go back into the mountain of the Lord and would offer atonement for their sin, so that his attention might be engaged and forgiveness granted.

But first I went into my tent and closed it. And Caleb brought my meal, and I listened to the sounds of the encampment settling down. I refused to hear the crying of those whose men had been killed. I felt, now, as if my earlier self had been emptied into the reddened dust around the altar, as if my limbs had been cut off so that my life was pouring steadily away, endlessly, irretrievably.

XVIII

If I Now Have Found Grace

I knelt before the Lord, knowing what I must offer.

'Oh, this people', I said to him, speaking softly, my emotions dormant, my future uncertain, 'have sinned a great sin, and have made them gods of gold.'

Here I paused, remembering he had told me as much, and staring sightlessly at the sand and littered stones.

'Yet now, if thou wilt forgive their sin. . . .'

There was no answer. Only the awareness of a presence withdrawn, waiting afar off, and inscrutable.

'Yet now,' I repeated, 'if thou wilt forgive their sin. . . .' I hitched my robe about me. Even in my dereliction, the stones were sharp. I moistened my lips. 'And if not, blot me, I pray thee, out of thy book which thou hast written.'

The substitute victim. The horned goat. I knew a sudden desolation, seeing the endless desert unfolding its enmity beneath my driven feet.

The Voice, when it came, was implacable.

'Whosoever hath sinned against me, him will I blot out of my book.'

But they have repented, I assured him, and those who refused to give up the evil have been cut off. Even as you had willed, O Lord.

He was silent, and I asked myself whether indeed it was possible to recover from this thing which they – which we – had done. But were there not, always, the children? Surely they would be accounted innocent? Or would it not be until the third and fourth generation? For a moment I beguiled myself with the vision of a younger company, untainted. Though even this was uncertain. Then the Lord spoke once more.

'And now go,' he told me, 'lead the people unto the place of which I have spoken unto thee: behold, mine angel shall go before thee: nevertheless in the day when I visit, I shall visit their sin upon them.'

With this I had to be content. I did not understand about the day of the Lord's visitation, though I feared it. Also, I wanted the Lord himself to walk beside us, as he had done hitherto, not just his angel. Was this now too much to demand? I did not know. Later, it was to become all too apparent – but now, only a vague disturbance on the edges of my mind.

I left the Lord in a trance of great joy and greater relief, for as I went from his presence, he said to me: 'Hew thee two tables of stone like unto the first; and I shall write upon the tables the words that were on the first tables, which thou brakest. And be ready by the morning, and come up in the morning unto Mount Horeb, and present thyself there to me on the top of the mountain.'

His voice pursued me. 'And no man shall come up with thee, neither let any man be seen throughout all the mount; neither let the flocks nor herds feed before that mount.'

The next day I brought the new tablets to the Lord. It seemed that his wrath was somewhat abated, so, with the chilled iron warming a little in my soul, I let his words enter and become a part of me again.

'The Lord, the Lord,' I whispered, in unison with the pulsing fire, 'a God full of compassion and graciousness, slow to anger. . . .'

But was that so? Remembering the terrifying violence of his wrath, I thought not. Yet even so, had we the right to disparage the Lord? Was he not the Creator of the universe? The maker of all worlds, all times, all being? And were his ways not unfathomable to our restricted vision? Surely we could see but a fraction of his pattern – that small, precarious morsel which was our own short life-span – while he must balance the whole design upon his fingertips?

This was how I reasoned, knowing it to be a hard reckoning, but seeing the way now a little clearer. It was as if, in my people's disobedience, a sore had burst open and now the poison was out. So I made haste and bowed my head to the earth.

'If now,' I told him carefully, 'I have found grace in thy sight, O Lord, let the Lord, I pray thee, go in the midst of us; for it is a stiff-necked people: and pardon our iniquity and our sin, and take us for thine inheritance.'

There was silence; and I tried again.

'Yet they are thy people. . . .' My voice was soft yet stubborn.

Did I imagine it, or was there an answering gentleness? Had I pierced the Lord's armour? I could not be sure, yet there seemed a mildness within the cloud, and the flame died low. So I persisted, reminding the Lord, somewhat tartly, of his earlier resolution to send his angel into the Promised Land rather than to accompany us himself.

'If thy presence go not with me, carry us not up hence. For wherein now shall it be known that I have found grace in thy sight, I and thy people? Is it not in that thou goest with us, so that we be separated, I and thy people, from all the people that are upon the face of the earth?'

It seemed then that the Lord accepted the reasonableness of this argument, for at last I heard his voice.

'My presence shall go with thee, and I shall give thee rest.'

There came a pause, in which my ready rebellion gave way to thanksgiving. I shall give thee rest – it was as if he had touched me.

'I shall do this thing also that thou hast spoken,' the Voice continued, 'for thou hast found grace in my sight, and I know thee by name.'

It was then, in my foolishness, rising always above myself in moments of exaltation, that I begged to see his face – and was refused. How could I have challenged him thus? Of all his people, I might have shown humility, yet always my vanity competed with unquestioning compliance. Always I was to know mortification, always to become abashed at my own temerity. Yet he was not angry, and I knew a measure of relief. Indeed – and here, impulsively, I forgot my rashness – he knew me by name. So, my impetuous spirit rose and rejoiced.

'Behold,' he said to me, 'I make a covenant: before all thy people I shall do marvels, such as have not been wrought in all the earth, nor in any nation: and all the people among which thou art shall see the works of the Lord, for it is a terrible thing that I do with thee.'

Then he added, and I knew I had been right about Aaron: 'Take heed to thyself lest thou make a covenant with the inhabitants of the land whither thou goest, lest it be for a snare in the midst of thee.'

He spoke then about his own true covenant and how we might bring into being all that he had laid down, and he wrote upon the tablets the words of those ten commandments already made known to us and now, written in the heart, to be committed to the less fluctuating nature of stone. I remained in his presence as if reborn, aware of his promise. I took neither food nor drink, for his words had become my bread and his blessing my spring of water.

And when I came down the mountain for the last time, the cloud rolled back and the walls of Horeb were crowned with fire. I bore the tablets, still walking in this strange new peace.

Afterwards I was told that the skin of my face shone with the Lord's mercy, so that I moved within a covering of light. Aaron and all my people were afraid and would not come near me, but I called them and spoke to them and told them all that the Lord had said.

'And now, Israel . . .' – my voice caressed them – '. . . what doth the Lord thy God require of thee, but to fear the Lord thy God, to walk in his ways, and to love him, and to serve the Lord thy God with all thy heart and with all thy soul, to keep the commandments of the Lord, and his statutes, which I command thee this day for thy good?'

I raised the tablets high above my head, not this time for the breaking, but to let my people see the commandments of God, burned by his fire into the golden stones of Horeb.

'Behold,' I said, still pondering the immensity of his inscrutable dealings with this small people, 'unto the Lord thy God belongeth the heaven, and the heaven of heavens, the earth, with all that therein is.'

They were kneeling now, their faces stripped back to innocence.

'Only the Lord,' I emphasised, making no mention of that other god they had worshipped, 'only the Lord had a delight in thy fathers to love them, and he chose their seed after them, even you above all peoples, as at this day.'

A sigh of release issued from them, swelling to a breath of thanksgiving.

'As at this day,' I repeated, watching them closely. Then,

drawing a likeness, which they would easily understand, between their own need of moral purification and that fleshly covenant made by our forefather Abraham, I added: 'Circumcise therefore the foreskin of your heart, and be no more stiff-necked.'

I was standing now between the tablets of the Lord, they being balanced upon a shelf of yellow rock. The Lord's words poured through me.

'For the Lord your God, he is God of gods, and Lord of lords, the great God, the mighty, and the terrible.'

Yes, I thought, the terrible. Let us not doubt this. He is light and darkness compounded, and his power is both a smoke and a shining, while his love can destroy or heal. His love? Mankind may not easily abide the dreadfulness of his love, nor the light of his shining, nor the deeps of his compassion. He can but be approached in the silence of his waiting.

'To him shalt thou cleave,' I told them, 'and by his name shalt thou swear. He is thy praise, and he is thy God, that hath done for thee these great and terrible things, which thine eyes have seen.'

I looked them over, rank on rank, spread across the desert, pressed down as grains of sand into the stones.

'Thy fathers', I said gently, 'went down into Egypt with threescore and ten persons: and now the Lord thy God hath made thee as the stars of heaven for multitude.'

Stars of heaven? Grains of sand? What were we, containing both heaven and earth within our frail humanity? I know that I smiled upon them, my face transfigured by the light I bore within me. Then I veiled my face from their sight and went to my tent, bearing the tablets with me.

———— XIX ————

The Tent of Meeting

There came to us now a time of tranquillity such as I had never before experienced, spreading over the encampment as if the spirit of the Lord had penetrated every tent. I moved among my people softly, their lenient prophet returned, understanding that not only I, but all of us, had now found grace in the Lord's sight. The days and the months passed slowly in a quiet rhythm, each day with the sun's unremitting glare reflected off the scorching sand; each night with its bitter cold and the almost tangible darkness and the stars brilliantly clustering the desert sky. We learned the secret greenness of Horeb, where small valleys were shadowed and where herbs grew. There was a hum of contentment about the camp, and the children grew tough and agile and obedient.

And, beyond all else, we made the tent of meeting.

This was our daily work, our common devotion, building the tabernacle which was to be the core of our life, the centre of all being, that place round which the people of Israel might at last begin to find coherence. It became our hearth, our heart.

And my people, who had so eagerly given gold rings to the firing of the blood-stained calf, now brought, with equal celerity, their thousandfold offerings to the Lord God of Israel: gold and silver and brass; the blue woollens and the purple and the scarlet; the fine linen and the goats'-hair weaving. Those who had them, brought rams' skins dyed red; others gave their sealskins and still others their gifts of acacia wood. We received also, I and Aaron and his sons and all those of the tribe of Levi who were chosen by the Lord to serve him at the tent of meeting, offerings of oil for the lamps, as well as myrrh and sweet cinnamon, calamine and cassia and olive oil, to be mixed for the oil of anointing. For incense we took stacte and onycha and gabanum, mixed with frankincense and seasoned with salt. And we set the severest prohibitions about these holy things, so that the oils were reserved for the anointing of Aaron and his sons, while any who should make another kind of incense, remembering the worship of the golden calf and using it before the Lord, would be cut off from his people.

Finally each of the tribes, according to its own appropriate choice, brought us the required stones to be set for the priest's garment and for his breastplate which was to contain the people's judgement: the sardine, topaz and carbuncle; the emerald, sapphire and diamond; the jacinth, agate and amethyst; the beryl, onyx and the jasper.

The act of offering, as I insisted, was carried out soberly. The men brought their families' brooches and ear-rings, their signet-rings and other treasures – put now to a more holy use than the worship of the bull – and the women, governed by my domineering sister, became busy at spinning the blue and purple and scarlet wool and weaving both it and the heavier curtains of goats' hair.

We found a designer, Bezalel of the tribe of Judah. It was the Lord who chose him out (aptly, for his name signified 'The Lord's shadow'), telling me that he had filled the man with his spirit, making him wise and understanding and full of the knowledge of craftsmanship. So Bezalel was set to work in gold and silver and brass, cutting the stones for setting and carving the wood as the design dictated. There was also his assistant, a young man named Oholiab of the tribe of Dan, usefully expert in engraving and embroidery.

When all the work was done – it had taken a great many months – and when the separate pieces of the structure were placed ready, I saw that we should have a sanctuary which might easily be taken apart and carried on our journey. The Lord then told me what I must do, and I took Caleb and Joshua to help me, together with several of the young Levites. First, we reared up the shining golden framework of the tabernacle. Then, over this support, we hung the ten great curtains of blue and purple and scarlet, protecting them by the outer tent of rams' skins and sealskins. In front of this outer protection a large courtyard was cleared, fenced in with twenty pillars, each moulded with silver and having hooks of silver and sockets of brass. Upon these we hung curtains of fine linen. Then, in the open courtyard immediately before the tent, we placed the altar of sacrifice and the large brass vessels for ritual washing, while behind the alter we erected a screen against the door of entry into the tent. This was of blue and purple and scarlet like the interior curtains, raised on five pillars of acacia wood encased in gold.

When all this was done, I went alone into the inmost tabernacle. Here I placed the ark or chest which Bezalel had made to house the covenant of God. It was made of acacia wood, overlaid with gold and bore a golden crown. First, making myself ready and having washed my feet and my hands in the ritual vessels in the courtyard, I placed within the ark the two stone tablets I had brought down Mount Horeb. Upon the closed ark I rested the golden mercy seat from which the Lord had promised to commune with his people, and, on each side of the mercy seat, covering it with their wings so that it was entirely hidden, the two great golden cherubim. Next I set in order the flowering-branched candlestick and the seven lamps. Upon the gold table I placed the necessary gold vessels for the priest's use, and upon the small incense altar I placed ready the incense. Then, around the ark and shielding it from the gaze of those who must not dare approach, I placed the veil of the sanctuary. This was of blue and purple and scarlet, embroidered with cherubim, and it hung from four pillars overlaid with gold. When everything was prepared, I set upon the table the loaves of bread which were to be offered up, and I lighted the lamps and burned incense to the Lord and lighted also the almond-flowered candlestick.

For a long time I waited there, kneeling within the holy of holies, surrounded by the soft-gleaming walls of gold and covered over by the blue and the purple and the scarlet. I remembered, long ago, the Lord's voice from out of the burning bush. 'I AM THAT I AM,' he had said to me – unknowable, unfathomable, beyond all sight, above and below all sound, touch or tasting. Yet now he rested within the place we had built for him, and I rejoiced.

The light played over the gold wings of the cherubim, and as I watched, the Voice spoke to me from the mercy seat.

'I shall set my tabernacle among you,' It said, 'and I shall walk among you, and shall be your God, and ye shall be my people.'

The Voice entered me, and the place was filled to overflowing with the Lord's presence. 'Ye shall be holy,' It assured me, 'for I the Lord your God am holy.'

And still I knelt there, emptied of my own self-will, open to his incoming spirit, making myself available.

Later, I brought Aaron and his sons to the door of the tent of meeting, and there I washed their feet and their hands, and put upon them their priestly garments, Aaron bearing the crown of pure gold upon which was engraved the admonition *Holy to the Lord*. Next, I anointed him with oil, and sanctified him that he might minister to the Lord. I did the same for Aaron's sons, that his family should be an everlasting priesthood throughout all the generations.

All this was done openly, so that the people might see and understand the new order which was being celebrated. There was sacrifice, also, on the brass altar in the courtyard outside the tent of meeting, and this was done soberly as a necessary offering.

And so I finished the work which the Lord had laid upon me, and all the people gathered round, and the tent of meeting glowed like a many-sided jewel in the barren wilderness, and Aaron walked in dignity in his blue and purple and scarlet robe, his beard curled, the little golden bells tinkling among his embroidered pomegranates.

On this day, which was the first day of the first month of our second year, Horeb was finally bared to its habitual yellow rock – having housed the Lord within its high fastness, it now returned to a more natural glory. For the cloud, which had gone before us on our journey, came down from the mountain and covered the tabernacle, hovering over the Lord's testimony. It remained there in a tall shaft of smoke, soft as a bird's grey feathers. But in the night it shone like fire, a single pillar of energy.

It seemed now that the people understood the meaning of the cloud by day and the fire by night, seeing it resting over the place of the Lord. So when I went into the tent of meeting to speak with the Lord, all the people rose in homage, looking after me and standing each at the door of his own tent.

So it was to be always. And the Lord told me that whenever the cloud and the fire remained motionless over the tent of meeting, then we, the people of Israel, were to stay in that place where it had stopped, and might not go farther. But whenever the cloud arose and travelled before us, we were to move forward on our journey. Whether it were two days or two years that it brooded over the tabernacle, and whether it were two days or two years that it moved before us, we were to be obedient. It was our glory. The Lord's presence in the sight of Israel.

That first day, and during all of that first night, I refused to enter my tent. I knelt, hour by hour, on the blazing desert sand, cooled by the shadow of the pillar of cloud. And in the night I still knelt there, the desert's piercing cold tempered by the steadfast fire of the Lord's watchfulness. Our people moved discreetly around me, wary of intruding, while Joshua and Caleb shared the watch with me, stationed at a distance but ready to do my bidding.

I had come a long way from the time when I roamed the desert, empty in an empty land, yet listening in the end to the Voice from the burning bush. Not all of it had been as I could have wished it to be. But I had borne the testimony, and the place of the Lord was now established.

Was that not something? I hoped that it might be so.

XX

The Goat

We continued nearly seven weeks in the desert below Horeb, while the priests served God in the tent of meeting and the people were quiet and diligent. During this time I talked often with the Lord, his voice coming to me from the holy place of the mercy seat, veiled by the great golden wings of the cherubim. Everything he told me I repeated to my people, particularly the laws that touched on the various meats and other foods which were permitted, and the equally strict prohibitions on others which were not.

In the beginning, I could not understand why the Lord should be so inflexible about it all, seeing that we did not have so vast a choice in these matters anyway. I wearied of what I saw as the Lord's unreasonableness, believing no useful moral principle was involved and embarrassed by my people's lifted eyebrows as they suggested that it might be easier to follow such laborious regulations were we to have the opportunity. The desert, they remarked bluntly, scarcely provided a wide variety of delicacies.

Indeed, it was not until we settled at Kadesh for all the long years of our waiting that I began to understand how cunningly our special laws separated us from the surrounding pagan tribes and their dubious practices. Also, there grew up a daily pattern of self-discipline – indeed, of renunciation – which I could only approve. It was not until many years had passed that I also noticed, with surprise, how the people stayed healthier by observing these strange edicts, not so vulnerable to the diseases afflicting less abstemious eaters, and more able to endure adversity.

It was quiet during these weeks, as we lived under the shadow of Horeb, the days seeming to drift by slowly. Yet it was a time of preparation. I knew that it was a long march to our main resting-place at Kadesh-barnea, and that the way would lead through possibly hostile country. So I insisted on a count being made of all our men of twenty years and over who were able to go to war. But from this count I exempted the tribe of Levi, since the Levitic duty was not to engage in battle but to serve and guard the tabernacle, around which, when we camped, they would pitch their tents.

Thus, eventually, we developed a cohesive military force, and also a marching order, for I placed the Levites in the centre of a great square of people, they carrying the ark and the tabernacle and all the other sacred objects. To each of the tribes I gave a distinctive standard, remembering the battle with Amalek and how I had wished for something more heart-stirring than my shepherd's rod; remembering also that banner which had momentarily fluttered above the heads of Joshua and his men. The twelve tribes, each gathered around their standard, were to march in squared formation, three each to the north, the west, the east and to the south of the central company of Levites. As I soon realised, exempting the sons of Levi had left me short of a tribe, and since I knew it mattered to my superstitious people that we should maintain the sacred twelve, I divided the tribe of Joseph into two companies, calling them Ephraïm and Manasseh.

All this went well. Instead of a straggling rout, we now had a close-knit host, each tribe under its own banner, each knowing its exact position on the march, and each aware that all twelve tribes were the outer protection of their holy tabernacle.

I should have known that the march would not take place without trouble, but I was doubly grieved when that trouble came from within the servants of the tabernacle.

Nadab and Abihu, the two elder sons of Aaron, those whom I had never entirely trusted, were soon found to be foolish men, vain in their new priesthood and open to enticement. Perhaps they yearned for something more hazardous, more explosive than their patient daily routine before the Lord, for at last there came a day when each took his own censer and put fire into it and laid upon the fire a strange, prohibited incense, such as had been offered to the golden calf. Whether they did this because they were still hungry for the bull god, whether it was a rebellious act of childish temptation, each goading the other to risk his life, or whether they were drunk, we never knew. Only that the fire of the Lord flared up and, quenching the incense, destroyed also the two young priests.

In that moment I was softened as never before towards my brother, who railed at the Lord in despair and anguish at the loss. But with remembrance of the golden calf still so freshly before us, I forbade him his recriminations. 'This is what the Lord spake,' I pointed out, knowing it unwise to show my pity. And Aaron held his peace, acknowledging the necessary prohibition we had formed as a hedge about the use of incense.

I called two men who were our cousins and told them to take the bodies and place them outside the camp. So, with their coats wrapped about them, Nadab and Abihu were carried away.

Then I spoke again to Aaron and to Eleazar and Ithamar, his two remaining sons. 'Let not the hairs of your head go loose,' I told them, forbidding our usual mourning rituals, 'neither rend your clothes . . .' – adding the warning, in case the Lord should transfer his anger to them for excessive grieving and insufficient condemnation of this wickedness – '. . . that ye die not, and that he be not wrathful with the whole congregation.' Then, thinking that perhaps the desecration must surely have occurred because the two young men were drunk, I added: 'Drink no wine nor strong drink, thou, nor thy sons with thee, when ye go into the tent of meeting, that ye die not: it shall be a statement for ever throughout your generations. . . .'

I brooded for a moment, torn by their stolid grief, then reinforced the importance of our behaviour when we entered in to serve the Lord: '. . . that ye may put difference between the holy and the common, and between the unclean and the clean.'

I told them then, as I had so often told them before, knowing at least that Eleazar understood, how we were a people in process of becoming the one great instrument of the Creator's will, and that to the forging and tempering of an instrument fire was necessary, and that the fire – even though it brought death – might not be omitted in the proper making of such an instrument.

Then I advised Aaron and his sons how they should make atonement for what had been done. I indicated the sacrifices to be offered, including the goat to be slain and the goat to be driven out to bear the burden of our sin. Our sin. For I felt I was implicated.

Ceaselessly, as the preparations went forward, I asked myself how this thing could have happened; whether perhaps I had not been sufficiently painstaking in my teaching; whether I might indeed have shown more zest, winning the young men to an eager service of the Lord by a more simple affection than with my habitual austere counselling. Now it was done, and their bodies were cast out, and soon the animal carrying the burden of our sin would be cast out also. But was not I the true bearer of this sin? Which of us is clean? I asked myself. Would I not therefore perceive my own image within the yellow eyes of the victim?

So I took great pains, feeling it to be my own task, in seeking out the two goats myself, making sure that they were perfect in every way, waiting anxiously while Aaron cast the lot. And when it had fallen, and when Aaron had killed the goat of the blood offering, I faced the other that was left. And now I trembled in my soul. The animal stood meekly, its large head hanging, one foreleg pawing at the ground, but otherwise remaining patient and still. Then Aaron came to it and laid his hands upon its head, on that rough, wiry, bony prominence between the great back-curving horns, confessing over it the iniquity of Israel. And as he did this, the goat mildly arched its neck and looked at me, so that I saw myself within the sad affliction of its gaze. The holy and the common . . . the unclean and the clean. . . .

For a long moment the goat's innocence challenged me, and I shivered in the hot sun. Then a man stepped forward, taking it by a rope and leading it away beyond the camp: our sin, to be driven out. It went docilely, stepping with delicacy into the solitary lands, there to be taken by Azalel, the fallen angel-demon, at his will. And for a part of the way, even as one beneath a spell, I walked with it.

I think my people believed this to be a part of the ritual; that I would work some magic of my own so that the beast should not return. But I had no magic. In the end, all I did was to take the rope from the man's hands, and lead the goat across the desert to where the bush that had burned for me, shrunken now and splintered, still rattled a few dry leaves in the wind. And here, away from the sight of all my people, and with my tears falling into the goat's tangled hair, I loosed it from the rope. In sorrow and great dread and with a fierce compassion.

The creature took no notice – had indeed taken no notice beyond that one strange, acquiescent look as Aaron had laid iniquity upon it. Then it had recognised me: you and I are one, it had agreed, and nothing more remained to be acknowledged between us.

It moved forward as if it knew that it was outcast, and it went heavily as if burdened. But it did not turn back, and I watched it go, quietly, neatly, picking up its small hoofs with care among the sharp stones as if concerned not to dislodge whatever burden had been placed upon it.

'And he shall make atonement for the holy place,' I said, remembering the Lord's words about the priesthood, 'because of the uncleannesses of the children of Israel, and because of their transgressions, and all their sins.'

But I was not thinking of priestliness, only of this creature – that ancient emblem of our sin – which yet was guilelessly a part of God's creation and thus better fitted, perhaps, to bear our offences. Only the innocent might bear transgression. But also there was no innocence, and most certainly the goat was tainted with our fall. There remained the readiness, unresisting, to bear affliction. Perhaps, I thought, seeing myself horned and driven out, that might be sufficient. Perhaps, in the end, it was that bearing of affliction to which my people would be called.

Meanwhile, the goat would carry this burden now placed upon it, more worthy than I to carry iniquity.

'This is the law of the guilt offering,' I reflected, as the wind rose in a sudden gust of grit and sand, blotting out the last, slow-moving shadow of that meek creature. 'It is most holy.'

Then it was gone, gathered into the soft purple dusk. I stood there for a long time, motionless, yet moving ever with it and within it.

XXI

The Wilderness of Paran

It seemed unreasonable that a period of strengthening and peace should so often erupt into strife. The months we spent below Horeb, after the dark excesses of the golden calf, had been a time of recovery and growth. We had been given the law. We had become a people. We had shaped ourselves into a disciplined host. We had found, each one of us, our own place within the pattern of our common life. Above all, we had begun to understand what it meant to be free, no longer the slave-labourers of Egypt. I had looked into our future and imagined (with my usual and so often unjustified tendency towards an easy exaltation) our vast, sweeping, irresistible movement into the Promised Land, my people retaining their new vision, so that Israel would advance through the surrounding pagan tribes as the undeviating witness to the One God.

Indeed, when we left Horeb on the twentieth day of the second month of the second year, we marched in the precisely defined square I had laid down, and in spite of the shambling herds of beasts, in spite of the swaying carts piled high with our tents and all the inevitable, ill-packed litter of a great camp on the move, we preserved a controlled formation, setting forth in orderly, almost military cohesion.

At the beginning, the twelve standard-bearers were proud to flaunt their colourful banners, the men of each company marched singing, and the children stepped out with a solemn air of dedication, facing, we believed, towards a Promised Land which might well be very near. Only eleven days to Kadesh (though in fact we took much longer), and then? Our voices lifted joyfully over the dry desert as the prospect unfolded of green lands and a multitude of little springs.

This time I walked behind my people. For now we had a guide to lead us through this new wilderness: Hobab, the son of Jethro, sent to me by my father-in-law. Not that it had been easy to persuade Hobab. Disdainful of his task but dutiful to his father, he had joined our ranks unwillingly. I had appraised him with a sinking heart, finding no likeness to my loved Jethro (for certainly, all his children appeared singularly lacking in Jethro's even-tempered wit and wisdom) and doubting if we would make much use of this guarded, resentful man. 'We are journeying', I told him, 'unto the place of which the Lord said: "I shall give you": come thou with us, and we shall do thee good: for the Lord hath spoken good concerning Israel.'

But he had jerked his chin fiercely, repudiating us, his black eyes flashing with dislike: 'I will not go.' His voice had been sullen.

I had waited then, anxious not to drive him into open hostility. Why this mulishness? I wondered. What was wrong? What had I done to displease him? I thought it could have been jealousy, because of the love his father bore me, and my mood softened towards him, so that I smiled – as indeed I had smiled in friendship throughout his stay. But it brought no response.

'I will depart to mine own land.' Again the surly dislike, the jutting chin, the rejecting hunch of a shoulder. 'And to my kindred,' he added with deliberate malice.

I sighed. My kindred. Meaning, not yours. Well, remembering Zipporah, perhaps I merited his distaste. But we needed him, and so I had tried again, ignoring his boorish ill-humour.

'Leave us not, I pray thee . . .' – and I had stretched out my hands to him in the age-old gesture of fellowship – '. . . forasmuch as thou knowest how we are to camp in the wilderness, and . . .' here I attempted a dry cajoling – '. . . and thou shalt be to us instead of eyes.'

He shifted, then, uncomfortable, embarrassed, perhaps hearing in my voice something of his father's amused affection.

'And it shall be, if thou go with us,' I added, sensing that there must be something of gain for him in our transaction, 'yea, it shall be, that what good soever the Lord shall do unto us, the same shall we do unto thee.'

So. A touch of cupidity, a touch of pride, even perhaps

compunction for his ungraciousness: all this seemed to turn the uncertain balance, so that Hobab had agreed, half-heartedly, to lead us into the wilderness of Paran. Friendship with him was more than I could hope for. Therefore I handed him over to march with Joshua at the head of our host, carefully avoiding my captain's raised eyebrows and the humorous glint in his all-seeing eyes.

So we had moved out, and I was glad that I remained in the rear. Not because of Hobab, but because of Horeb. I turned back often, watching the mountain's yellow walls lose shape and colour as our direction changed and the days wore on. Nothing, now, would be quite the same, I thought, even though the Lord travelled among us where the cloud rested over Aaron and the tabernacle. My task now was no longer to receive the law but constantly to interpret it, binding it into my people's hearts so that they ceased to stray.

Within my own heart I held the image of Horeb's bowl of light, where the Lord had waited for me and where I had listened to his voice and attended to his will. Then, in a time which was timeless, I had been contained within that shining cup. Now, it was as if the cup rested within my bosom, to be delicately sustained, so that I did not spill the light which brimmed over it. So I watched as the miles stretched out between us, and Horeb's timelessness was exchanged for the monotonous drive of the daily march. For several weeks the mountain compelled me, a spun thread which joined me to its secret and most holy places. But the thread wore thin, and there came a day, with Horeb forever out of sight, when, like a sigh, it parted and I was free of it. Free of it? Yes, for I had to look outward, not back.

During those nights when we camped in the wilderness of Paran, the tabernacle swiftly erected and the priests serving the Lord and the pillar of fire pulsing gently above the mercy seat, I discovered that no peace was ever likely to be lasting.

There was Joshua. Perhaps, in his devotion to me, he resented the distance which necessarily lay now between us, Caleb acting as go-between, even though he, Joshua, was now in deed, if not as yet by sanctification, the obvious commander of the host. He grew churlish in this new situation, converting his touchy jealousy into flares of anger, supposedly protective of me. At night, he became exceedingly busy about the camp, bringing me rumours I had already heard and did not need, and pretending great indignation on my behalf over a number of small matters. There were two men, harmless enough, who went among the people making prophecy. It seemed to me that even though they were unorthodox the spirit truly rested upon them, and I was unwilling to restrain them.

But Joshua glowered darkly, his handsome face wearing too much of Aaron's bluster to be agreeable. 'My lord Moses,' he cried, striking his fist into his palm, then striding around my tent so that his adornments jangled, 'forbid them! Forbid them!'

I looked at him consideringly, seeing his temper; seeing also his trembling lip and all the signs of uncontrolled emotion in this now maturely aged man. I felt troubled by the violence of his devotion. But I answered him gently, for I loved him well. 'Art thou jealous for my sake?' I asked. I kept my voice warm, yet thought it wise to permit a trace of amusement, so that he stopped in his striding and hung his head, looking up at me from under his thatch of rough black hair with an expression of doglike fidelity.

'Would God', I added, 'that all the Lord's people were prophets, that the Lord would put his spirit upon them.'

And so the matter ended, and Joshua came back into himself.

But there was still the old trouble over the sparseness of our desert fare. The people wearied, as I had known they would, of the endless supply of manna, and lusted after a more enticing diet. They came after me during the march and then each night as we camped, even grasping at my garments and daring to stand in my way to block my tent. 'Who shall give us flesh to eat?' they argued, while the women wept covertly but with determination.

My sister Miriam waylaid me boldly. 'We remember the fish which we did eat in Egypt,' she accused me, and the women crept near, nodding at her and encouraging her wilfulness. 'For naught,' she added bitterly, as if that had made the taste even better and forgetting that the fish had indeed been paid for – with our freedom. She threw her arms wide, bracelets and anklets tinkling. 'The cucumbers,' she mentioned, while those around her groaned, 'and the melons, and the leeks, and the onions, and the garlic.'

Some of them wailed at this enumeration of past luxuries, and I forbore with difficulty to ask whether the very thought of onions had produced their tears.

'But now our soul is dried away,' came Miriam's virtuous grumble, 'and there is nothing at all. Nothing at all.' She gestured at the bowl of white grains her woman was carrying. 'We have nought save this manna to look to.'

Well, it was not lavish fare, that and the dried meat and the sparse milk. So I went into the tent of meeting and spoke with the Lord.

But he was angry. Unreasonably so, I decided, meeting his anger with my own in a surge of desperation. For I was weary of being hounded night and day by a murmuring people who would not let me be.

'Wherefore hast thou evil entreated thy servant?' I cried, watching the dangerous wreaths of smoke which coiled about the mercy seat, but caring not at all in my indignation. 'Wherefore have I not found favour in thy sight, that thou layest the burden of all this people upon me?'

Yes, indeed. This was the heart of the matter. Even though we had our judges and our elders and our captains, I alone must carry – as Jethro had pointed out – the full weight of the Lord's dealings with my people. I considered this, kneeling there amid the smoke. It was, I knew, too much to bear.

Something in me then broke apart. I bowed my head and wept before the Lord. I, whose face had shone with his glory. I, who carried his light within me.

'Have I conceived all this people?' I complained. 'Have I brought them forth, that thou shouldst say unto me, Carry them in thy bosom, as a nursing father carrieth the sucking child, unto the land which thou swarest unto their fathers?'

I rocked to and fro, my beard wet, my face plunged into my hands. In the midst of my wretchedness, even as I wept, I could see myself from afar, standing outside my body, aghast at such a demonstration of childishness. Why? I shouted. Why was it thus? Had the spring of my endurance broken, along with the breaking of that thread which had bound me to Horeb? Could it be so simple? So profound?

I thought of Jethro, always equable, always contained, always decisive, but no longer with me and not in any case the bearer of this terrible burden. I thought of Joshua, contrasting his brisk, unquestioning efficiency with my own uncertainties, my greying head; my greying visage. The shrivelled prophet, only a husk now, and occupied with problems of the cooking-pot where before he had walked the camp in conversation with the Lord, and the people had recognised this and fallen at his feet.

Was it not weakness but a consuming sin to regard with envy those now younger and stronger than I and better fitted to lead? So much jealousy, it seemed. Joshua. With that anger on my behalf which yet was directed against me, together with all those who would come near me. Hobab. Jealous of his father's love for me, and consorting daily with Gershom and Eliezer. Yes, my sons. Jealous that I was the honoured prophet while their mother remained forgotten in her father's tent. Aaron and Miriam. Still watchful to press for greater advantage should my step falter. And my people. My people.

I returned to the cooking-pot, thrusting it furiously at the Lord. His affair. His worry. Had he not spoken endlessly on such matters? So. Let him then attend to it.

'Whence should I have flesh to give to all this people? For they weep unto me, saying, Give us flesh, that we may eat.'

There was silence. Perhaps the Lord also found it wearisome. But I could not stop myself. 'I am not able', I shouted at him, 'to bear all this people alone, because . . .' – and I clutched in my madness at the golden edge of the incense table, remembering Nadab and Abihu, waiting and half wishing for a blaze of fire to consume my bones – '. . . because it is too heavy for me.'

I looked defiantly towards the mercy seat. 'Too heavy for me,' I repeated, adding with a cold passion of defeat, 'And if thou deal thus with me, kill me, I pray thee. . . .'

Yes, even as the Egyptians, even as the Amalekites, even as those unregenerate of my people who had danced before the golden calf. For was I not one with my people? Was I not engrafted on to them? Was not their sin my sin? And why should I be exempt because of my own peculiar authority?

'Kill me,' I repeated valiantly, my soul beginning to tremble, feeling the light now faded within me, quenched in my bitterness. 'Kill me, I pray thee, out of hand, if I have found favour in thy sight.'

Yes, grant me that mercy. My privilege. Because he knew me by name, because I had found grace. Therefore he must treat with me. His obligation: to kill me, or to lift the burden. Those were my conditions.

I fell to the ground. 'And let me', I entreated, 'not see my wretchedness.'

After this, I lay for a time as one dead. But the Lord had not struck me down and presently I heard his voice. It seemed, in my near-delirium, to be the voice of Jethro, wise and kind, compassionate and loving. At first, in my stupor, I was unable to distinguish the meaning. But it went on, inexorably, sharpening a little as my own voice so often did, yet always with that note of grace. It was clearly no word of pity. That much became plain. Simply the Lord's expedient dealing with an out-of-hand predicament.

'Gather unto me seventy of the elders of Israel,' he was telling me, 'whom thou knowest to be the elders of the people, and officers over them; and bring them unto the tent of meeting, that they may stand there with thee.'

The smoke had departed. The lamps burned steadily. The golden wings of the cherubim protected the mercy seat of the Lord.

'And I shall come down and talk with thee there.' The Voice caressed me, bringing peace to my soul. 'And I shall take of the spirit which is upon thee,' said the Voice, 'and shall put it upon them; and they shall bear the burden of the people. . . .'

Was I to be cast out? Driven, small-hoofed, meek-necked, across the wilderness?

'And they shall bear the burden of the people with thee,' concluded the Voice, answering my fear. 'With thee, that thou bear it not thyself alone.'

And so it was done. The strange thing which had broken within me, and which I did not understand, was seemingly bound up again, and I no longer walked alone.

The Lord, as was his habit, punished those who had despaired of his promises by hankering after Egypt. He sent us a gift: thousands upon thousands of quails, succulent, delicious. Upon these the people gorged themselves till they sickened, and because the quails had not been properly prepared, there came a plague into the camp and many died.

But perhaps it was not the Lord's doing? Perhaps the quails would have come anyway. Only, I remembered that the Lord had threatened this thing.

— XXII —

The Cushite Woman

Perhaps my outburst before the Lord had not, after all, been caused by the burden I must bear (though indeed it was heavy), nor even by my fear of all those contemptuous (or so it seemed to me) of my rigidity and my often uncontrolled explosions of wrath.

Looking back, I still could observe within myself the arrogant, solitary young prince, belonging to no people and to no place. In that time I had known rejection; my authority had been toppled, I had become an outcast in the wilderness. There, I had learned independence, a toughening. But it had been a friendless experience, my mind shaped by the inarticulate desert and liable to cringe at overbearing voices – my tongue always betraying that double self and its uncertainties, my mind woefully ready to accept both sides of a dispute. I had come to Zipporah too late, or maybe too early, finding and indeed giving no warmth, so that we knew little of each other but the body's needs. Strange that Jethro's children should house such quick resentments. But then I did not match up to the father, so that the children must soon have discovered that my docility cloaked weakness.

(Yet I had been chosen?)

I considered the long years in Egypt, preparing my people for their exodus. There, I had come to some sort of equilibrium, giving myself entirely to the Lord, becoming his messenger, and recognisably bearing his holy spirit. Even Pharaoh had seen this, tempering his naturally despotic inclinations because, beneath deep layers of inherited superstition, he feared me. No, let me not think that thought. He feared the Lord God of Israel, unwillingly acknowledging a power beyond anything he had ever known.

As for my people, they had not then been put to the test. One day, but not too soon and not too uncomfortably, we shall leave our serfdom behind us. Meanwhile we are secure within our bonds. We can listen respectfully to our new prophet, accepting with suitable awe his edifying admonitions. We need come to no decisions, take no thought for the morrow. We can pray earnestly for the Promised Land, since there is little likelihood of our starting on such a journey for some considerable time.

And I? Even then, moving among my people and filled with God's fire, I had no close human ties. Wife and children had been banished to Jethro – I, always being impatient of their claims and shunning involvement. Only the vast, indefinable mass of my people could be tolerated, none of them close enough to matter, and I, therefore, neatly detached from the frictions of daily living.

Then there had come the desert journey, unexpected and even unwelcome after years of procrastination. The terrible unwillingness of my people, their bitterness, their reproaches; in the course of which I had struggled with them, and in the struggling had withered a little, turning dry even as the burning bush had turned dry. A man cannot hold on to exaltation, and when it has leaked away, that, too, is recognised.

Yet there had been the revelation upon Horeb. Its holiness and our evil. In the end the glory of the Lord had outweighed disaster, and my people had become more or less obedient. So perhaps it had not been altogether wasted, this unending battle within myself, the desire for gentleness, the ready plunge into irritation. After all, were my people not children also? I wondered now whether very much could be done with them – this slave-accustomed generation. Should I not rather look to the children to become the forged instrument of the Lord's purposes?

Meanwhile, unable to accommodate myself to my people's superstition, and avoiding (most certainly with alarm) the suffocation of being bound to any one individual, I knew myself now to be alone. Pierced through, since those dreadful moments of my wretchedness before the Lord, with a hunger I scarcely understood. A hunger of the body, but also a loneliness of the spirit. There were women, plenty of them in that teeming camp, but this was not what I wanted. I needed something closer and more durable. I needed, for the first time, and in my increasing years, to find refuge, to find – these being accepted – that chains do not always constrict.

Yet, I reasoned, was it not too late? And (rather more important than my suddenly erupting needs) was it not a rash thing for the acknowledged prophet of Israel to look upon a woman? I knew my people. Brimming with ordinary human lusts, they expected the messenger of God to serve as their perfection, thus leaving them free to be human. Even the priests of Israel were allowed their small peccadilloes. But the man who bore the Lord's fire was, for them, no longer a man. Nor might he behave as a man. This I knew and I accepted. I was to be holy, set inconsolably apart. But also, as ever, I knew myself to be at the mercy of my unsatisfactory, intractable self-will, the stubborn determination to do just that thing I intended to do whatever the outcome. So, in the end, I found the woman I needed. Or rather, she was placed in my way, for I had not sought her out.

There were many small companies travelling with us, attaching themselves to one tribe or another and journeying under our protection across the wilderness. Among them had been a Cushite family. They came from a distant land, far south of Egypt, a dark-skinned people, so dark that I had heard them called by another name, which meant 'people with burnt skins'. Yet they were not burnt, and their darkness recalled the still, carved figures of Egypt. During the time between Elim and our present camp, the mother had died of sickness, and the father had been killed in our battle with the Amalekites. There had been a boy, but it seemed he had disappeared, perhaps straying too far from the camp, or joining with another group of travellers and going back towards his own country. There was left only a young woman, who became handmaid to a daughter-in-law of Aaron.

So I saw her often about the camp. My Cushite woman.

Looking back, I cannot now describe her features, even though they were immutably carried in my heart. Certainly she was in no way beautiful to look upon, but she was soft and gracious and gentle, with a smile that reached to my heart. For a short time I followed her daily, knowing what must be, yet knowing also that it should not be. She was aware of me with a quiet pleasure, not seeming to notice my greying hairs, though her own were black. Later it would be said of her that she had seduced me, puffed up with desire to become the wife of the prophet. But that was not so.

In my stubbornness, I married her, forgetting Zipporah, forgetting my sons, forgetting – yes – forgetting Miriam. I took her into my tent and lay with her in astonishment of joy and release. She was very young, and her body, so black and so tender, had a bloom upon it as of dark, shining stone.

She is within me, I discovered, and I am in her bones. And this was so, for in a strange way and for the short time that we were allowed to be together, we became one being, each supplying that separate part which the other lacked. It was a binding of two persons into one, as if each had been but a half of what had been intended, so that – the two halves now come together – the entire, completed self was disclosed.

She spoke seldom – for our speech differed – but her eyes were always upon me, gentle and welcoming. Yet she did not set me upon an unattainable pillar as some of my people were wont to do. Simply, she bestowed a continuing acceptance. I could not say she was knowledgeable about many matters, but then I had long since forgotten my own court learning, remaining – as she was – schooled by the desert silence. She had, instinctively, a right judgement, and the habit of slow reflection. She had also, more profoundly, a subtle, archaic wisdom.

What did I find in her? Strangely, in view of the years between us, I prized most of all among the many facets of her being, that tenderness which, as a child, I had longed for but never inspired. Her body became my shelter, my fortress – she holding my self within her capable hands and healing, if only for some fleeting moments, my uncertainties.

Perhaps it would not have remained so. A prophet-leader may not detach himself from those who would, in dreadful innocence, consume him, even as the beast upon the altar is consumed. And the sacrifice must be unblemished. This I knew. But in the unaccustomed grace of becoming accepted, so much is easily forgotten. Even the Lord. This also I recognised, as did my Cushite woman. The future lay, inevitably, as a desert between us; but if she was afraid of it, she did not let me see her fear.

It was Miriam who ended it, choosing, as she thought, the right moment to reduce me to ordinary clay. Miriam, and of course Aaron, aided by Hobab's mischievous tongue. Not that

Hobab was necessary. I remembered the hasty whisperings in Egypt when Miriam had encouraged Aaron's jealousy. Seeing them together now, with Hobab's added influence and with Gershom and Eliezer as living witnesses to my neglect of Zipporah, I saw that there could be only one end. Saw, but would not see.

I knew also that, while I should suffer loss, more loss than I had ever experienced, Miriam could not win this battle. She sought nothing less for Aaron than my own place, but this was not, for any of us, disposable. In forgetting this, they overreached themselves.

'Hath the Lord', she stormed, publicly denouncing me for taking a wife, 'indeed spoken only with Moses?' She looked about her in triumph, drawing the people into her net. 'Hath he not spoken also with us?'

There came a nodding of heads, eager, avaricious. Yes, also with us. Not only Moses. We, we are the whole priestly people. But the choosing of the mouthpiece rested with the Lord. How could she have forgotten?

It was then that we were called out before the tent of meeting, I and Aaron and Miriam, with the people crowding as near as they dared, and Hobab lurking at a prudent distance. The smoke from the mercy seat billowed furiously out of the tabernacle.

'Hear now my words,' cried the Voice, in a passion of anger. I listened with a curious detachment, yet also with gratitude. Let it be swift, O Lord God of Israel, I told myself, prepared for the inevitable end; let it not delay. 'If there be a prophet among you,' the Voice persisted, 'I the Lord shall make myself known unto him in a vision, I shall speak with him in a dream.'

Miriam defiant. Aaron faltering. In the background, Hobab indifferent, yet certainly wishing himself elsewhere. And my sons impatient, sullen, reluctant. I saw them all as standing outside reality.

'My servant Moses is not so,' announced the Lord, demolishing the accusations against me. 'He is faithful in all mine house; with him will I speak mouth to mouth. . . .'

Yes, this the people heard. As it was intended they should. My heart unfroze a little.

'Even manifestly, and not in dark speeches. . . .'

Aaron glancing uneasily at Miriam, she upright still and boldly insolent. Should they not kneel?

'And the form of the Lord shall he behold: wherefore then were ye not afraid to speak against my servant, against Moses?'

I could see the people backing away in a wave of terror, while Miriam and Aaron remained as if struck to stone, the cloud veiling them from our sight. When it cleared, a different Miriam stood revealed, a bleached and whitened thing shining with a leprous-tainted skin, her savage beauty gone. She swung her head this way and that, cowering now before the Lord, and the people witnessed her despoiling.

As for Aaron, he was left untouched. Perhaps the Lord accepted him as Miriam's tool. But then I remembered that he was already under proscription following the wickedness of his sons, forbidden to enter the tabernacle at his own will, lest he should also die. Perhaps the Lord judged his situation precarious enough without meriting that final penalty.

Then a curious thing happened. Seeing Miriam so white-marked and afflicted, Aaron hid his face in his hands, rocking to and fro as if he himself had been defiled. 'Oh my lord,' he cried.

Yet he spoke not to the God of our people but to me, his brother – he, the High Priest of Israel, the anointed servant of the Lord, turning for judgement not to his God but to me. I recoiled from him in horror, aware of the Lord's silence, aware of what it could mean.

'Oh my lord,' he said again, more gently now, 'lay not, I pray thee, sin upon us, for that we have done foolishly, and for that we have sinned.'

Then, in his love for Miriam, for indeed he loved her, he knelt at her side, stretching out his hands. To me.

'Let her not, I pray, be as one dead, of whom the flesh is half consumed as he cometh out of his mother's womb.'

In the midst of my consternation, and with the growing weight of a great emptiness upon me, I cringed from Aaron's words. Must I, then, give the judgement? Must I be the one to lay sin upon them? I, their brother? Appalled by such a dreadful requirement, disgusted and ashamed and shrinking, I turned to the Lord. But he remained silent, awaiting, it seemed, my response, and prepared to abide by whatever it might be.

So I gathered myself together, trembling in hope of his mercy, yet knowing in my cold and frightened heart that, in the end, even if Aaron and Miriam were pardoned, there would be a price to pay and that I and no other must pay it for them. 'Heal her, O God,' I begged, taking my place beside her, taking her ashy fingers within my own, and trying to mean these words and to shut out the knowledge of her cruelty. Then I knelt and laid my head upon the ground. 'Heal her, O God, I beseech thee.'

And still there was silence, as the smell of corruption assailed my nostrils, and the Lord weighed up my plea, passing his judgement upon my judgement. Presently he spoke, but his voice was sharp and dissatisfied. 'If her father had but spit in her face,' he responded, dwelling upon the laws of defilement, 'should she not be ashamed seven days? Let her be shut up without the camp seven days, and after that she shall be brought in again.'

Did he think me a fool, when I had held them – their malevolence, their jealousy – within my hand? I could not tell.

Miriam was taken away in shame and placed naked in a small hut outside the encampment, remaining alone, her garments having been burned. We stayed in that place until her penance was done and she was brought in again to her own tent, healed of her transgression.

During those seven days the camp was quiet. Aaron went about his ritual with an anxious face, afraid maybe that the Lord might notice him and decide to afflict him also. Hobab kept his distance, preparing hastily to take his departure. My two sons were not to be seen. As for Caleb and Joshua, both of whom had accepted my taking a wife, being always deferential and considerate towards her, they rejoiced rather blindly at what they felt to be a happy issue out of but a slight disturbance. And my Cushite wife lay in my arms as before.

Yet it was not the same. Certainly the bond between us was strengthened so that we brought to each other not only the quick rush of delight but a deep well of contentment, from which we drew clear water. But our relationship now subtly changed, so that while the delight remained, we would more often cling together in a new mood of solemnity, as of sorrow accepted and turned into something unbreakable.

She was wiser than I. Looking back, I can see that she had made her decision and was but biding her time, making sure that it could not be whispered in the camp that I had banished her in fear of my people's disapproval. Making sure that I should be left unstained.

We moved out of the camp at the end of the seven days, and Miriam kept herself apart – a sister diminished by her affliction and knowing at last that neither she nor Aaron would ever wrest from me that which was solely the Lord's to give or to withhold.

So, with everything arranged and the host marching in our usual squared formation, we departed across the desert on the next stage of our journey, and it was not until we camped that night, with the cooking-pots ready and the myriad small fires burning, that I went to my own quarters and found my Cushite woman gone.

The tent was empty, no vestige of her presence remaining. The sheepskins and the woven bed-linen had been piled in a corner by an alien hand. For a moment I stood there, swaying a little. Then I fell, striking the ground like a tree falling – but endlessly, endlessly, and lying there as if the whole weight of Horeb pressed upon me.

She left no message, left nothing for me to remember her by, and though we searched the camp I found no trace of her. Later I recalled the great caravan that had passed us during the day, going in the other direction and halting to watch us through the turmoil of dust and sand made by our host. It had been journeying west and north towards the string of oases by the Sea of Reeds, eventually to make its way into Egypt. She must certainly have joined them, slipping away unobserved. She would travel with them, back along the way she had come, silent as ever, unobtrusive, competently making herself useful among the women of the various families and steadily putting an irrecoverable distance between her heart and mine. Perhaps she already bore my child. I should never know.

She had been the stronger, having seen that a prophet must stand alone. I did not recover her. Indeed, knowing why she had done this thing, I did not try, refusing to let Joshua ride hastily after the now far-distant caravan. The thing was done. And, having cut herself from me, she would have seen my attempt to regain her as a betrayal. Nor would she, I knew, have returned.

So I shut myself away, while the cloud remained motionless above the mercy seat and the camp rested. And for the next seven days and nights I mourned my wife as if she were dead. I wore the sackcloth, sitting as was customary in my tent upon the ground and placing earth and dust upon my head. But I could not weep.

Thus I made it clear to my people that I had lost the wife of my heart, and they, sensitive to my grieving, left small tributes beside the tent. Perhaps I drew nearer to them because of what had taken place. Yet, when I came forth from the empty tent on the eighth day, I looked about me and knew that I was alone.

XXIII

The Stoning

Something hardened in me at that time. It was not as she would have wished it to be, but I could not stop myself. Perhaps, had she continued beside me, I might have retained meekness but, because she had been taken, I kept my wound green, becoming more rather than less remote, readier at condemnation, sharper in punishment.

In the distant future, there would be acts of which I would be ashamed. They would spring out of my present bitterness and out of my lifelong awareness of deficiency, now more than ever unmanageable. These future infamies, always to be excused by their supposed necessity, were before me at this hour. I knew already that I would order the war against Midian: this was as clear to me as if, even now, I had called up my forces. I would tell my people, and myself, that the Lord must avenge himself because the Midianite immorality had infected our own people. And, since men find the sanctioning of their natural aggressiveness irresistible, I would be eagerly obeyed.

Well, war may become unavoidable, but was it unavoidable, afterwards, that I should order the killing of all those women, our captives, who had lain with men? What, in that future, would so move me? Would I be nursing a long hatred of every woman who had known a man? Would I then be taking a twisted retribution on my Cushite woman for depriving me of that solace, seeing her face imprinted upon all their faces?

And the children. Yes, I would suffer the female children to live, but every male child I would order to be killed. In this present time, after my Cushite woman's going, I paced the fringes of the camp, gazing into the wilderness and wrapping my sourness round me like a cloak. Everywhere, upon the shining, sun-bright rocks, upon the dark, strapped heads of palms and within the placid mirror of our oasis, I saw the future evidence of my cruelty. Their eyes. The patient, uncomplaining eyes of small boys, aware that they were about to die, knowing nothing of why this thing must be, but knowing certainly that they would like to live. Were Hobab's eyes like theirs, when he had been young? And my sons? Might not my sons' eyes, had I but kept the boys beside me, have regarded me with that same liquid gaze? Perhaps, I thought, ceaselessly probing, perhaps I would kill those Midianite boys to rid myself of jealousy and guilt.

And Jethro? Was not Jethro a priest of Midian? And would I fight against his people? Now, in the hot sun of our encampment, I shuddered at my future deeds, struggling to deny them yet knowing beyond doubt that I would do these things.

There would be other acts of shame. The self-righteous destruction of those who served other gods or who were dilatory regarding the Lord God of Israel. The permission, so promptly given, to take the backslider and stone him with stones. Did I so resent my own burden of purity that I had to avenge myself on those who slipped and fell beside me?

This was no light matter, and I carried the canker within me from that eighth day when I came out from my tent of mourning. These things I would do, one by one, deserted by former meekness and growing a crust over the soft underbelly of my mind. The visions haunted me. They came too near – no longer affirmations of my people's future in time far distant, but the careful, watching eyes of children I myself would kill.

Yet also I returned from my mourning with eagerness to serve the Lord – even, let it be said, with a certain obscure relief (how could this be?) that I was no longer encumbered. . . .

It was in the wilderness of Paran that the Lord first gave us intimations of the Promised Land. 'Send thou men,' he told me, as I stood before the mercy seat, 'that they may spy out the land of Canaan, which I give unto the children of Israel: of every tribe of their fathers shall ye send a man, every one a prince among them.'

So I called the men to me, including, of course, Caleb and Joshua. I went with them outside the camp, directing the few unreliable guides we could muster in default of Hobab, who had remained discreetly absent from the day Miriam went to her place of confinement. 'Get you up this way by the south,' I said to them, 'and go into the mountains: and see the land, what it is; and the people that dwelleth therein, whether they be strong or weak, whether they be few or many.'

I gave them precise instructions: 'And what the land is that they dwell in, whether it be good or bad; and what cities they be that they dwell in, whether in camps, or in strongholds; and what the land is, whether it be fat or lean, whether there be wood therein, or not. . . .' I looked around our dry desert, grimacing at the small, dry bushes. 'And be ye of good courage,' I exhorted them, fearing lest they might falter in these strange places and among unfriendly people, 'and bring of the fruit of the land.' For I knew it was the time of the first ripe grapes.

So they left us, journeying, as I learned later, from the wilderness of Zin to Rehob and Hamath until they came to Hebron and then to the valley of Eshcol, where they cut down grapes and pomegranates and figs, stringing them on long poles which they balanced on their shoulders, carrying them two by two.

They returned after forty days, reporting their findings to a tense and anxious people. Why so anxious, I wondered to myself. Always, it seemed, they acted as if threatened by any new thing. Yet living in tents in a dry desert on dry food was surely no great satisfaction, and should they not be eager to enter this last stage of their journey to the Promised Land? But no, they muttered restlessly, even eyeing the returned travellers as if they were strangers bringing dangerous news and therefore to be shunned.

'We came unto the land whither thou sentest us,' the men began, standing with Aaron and me on the raised flooring from which we always spoke, and regarding the people, in their turn, circumspectly. 'And surely it floweth with milk and honey; and this is the fruit of it.'

They displayed the grapes and the pomegranates and the figs, but with a subtle air of repudiation, so that even the sight of these luxuries did not impress the people.

'Howbeit . . .' – and here their words came quickly, the telling of the bad news seeming to accord better with their mood than the telling of the good – '. . . the people that dwell in the land are strong, and the cities are fenced, and very great: and moreover. . . .'

They poured out a confusing tale of a land occupied to the hilt: Amalekites in the south, Hittites, Jebusites and Amorites in the mountains, with the Canaanites dwelling by the sea and along the river of Jordan.

I watched these men carefully, seeing them gain assurance in the telling of their perils, flushed with remembered fear and glad of the people's ready response. I watched also how Joshua and Caleb grew angered and impatient at the way things were going. And suddenly, as the people swayed to and fro, uncertain but infected with a growing apprehension, Caleb strode forward, pushing his companions out of the way. 'Let us go up at once and possess it,' he cried, 'for we are well able to overcome it.'

Joshua stepped out with him, echoing his words, but even the commander of the host did nothing to quell the rising wave of protest.

The other ten captains now thronged about the two of them, shouting and waving their arms. 'We be not able to go up against the people,' they argued, 'for they are stronger than we.' The land, they said, was a land to eat up the inhabitants, like to our own wilderness. Even worse, they claimed, were the people – men of great stature, giants, against whom they had looked as grasshoppers.

At this, the people wailed aloud. There was confusion and moaning and a growing panic which swept like fire, and against which neither Joshua nor Caleb could prevail.

'Would God that we had died in the land of Egypt!' the nearer ones shouted. Once again the same recriminations, the same small spirit.

'Or would God', cried others, 'we had died in this wilderness.'

I could see them staring around and about, as if for the first time seeing our desert, against which, during these years, they had, as children, shut their eyes.

'Because the Lord hated us,' they shouted, 'he hath brought us forth out of the land of Egypt, to deliver us into the hand of the Amorites to destroy us.'

The elders nodded sagely, gaining strength from each other.

'Whither are we going up?' they demanded. 'Our brethren have made our hearts to melt, saying, The people are greater and taller than we; the cities are great and fenced up to heaven; and moreover we have seen the sons of the Anakim there.'

I took my place beside Joshua and Caleb. 'Dread not,' I said persuasively, 'neither be afraid of them. The Lord your God who goeth before you, he will fight for you, according to all that he did for you in Egypt before your eyes; and in the wilderness, where thou hast seen how that the Lord thy God bare thee, as a man doth bear his son, in all the way that ye went, until ye came unto this place.'

'And wherefore', cried the elders, brandishing their fists at us, 'doth the Lord bring us unto this land, to fall by the sword?'

'Yet in this thing', I replied, 'ye did not believe the Lord your God, who went before you in the way, to seek out a place to pitch your tents in, in fire by night, to show you by what way ye should go, and in the cloud by day.'

But they would not listen. 'Our wives', they said furiously, 'and our little ones shall be a prey. Were it not better for us to return to Egypt?'

There followed an awkward silence, their present fear contending with the even more fearful imaginings of a return across the desert. But then they rallied, some of them advancing on Joshua where he stood, raised above them, arms disdainfully folded. 'Let us make a captain,' cried the foremost, spitting on Joshua's feet, 'and let us return to Egypt.'

The cry was taken up, echoing around the tents: 'A captain . . . make a new captain . . . let us return . . . let us return to Egypt . . . return to Egypt!'

The sound of their voices came as a deep roaring, exultant yet remorseless as the sea. It held the ferocity of ultimate repudiation, the declaration of a united, insubordinate will.

I listened. It was a terrible sound, an inhuman bellowing, as of wild animals, and in that moment Aaron and I fell submissively before the people and hid our faces from them. Capitulation? Yes. I knew myself unable any longer to control them. They were controlling me, and I was now their puppet.

Yet Joshua and Caleb, though rending their garments in grief and dismay, persisted. 'The land', they shouted, scarce heard above the tumult, 'which we passed through to spy it out, is an exceedingly good land.'

Joshua raised his arms, standing resolute, and for a moment the frenzy died away. 'If the Lord delights in us, then he will bring us into this land, and give it unto us.' He spoke deliberately, his fierce eyes roving among the people, compelling them. 'A land', he added, disregarding their sullen humour, 'which floweth with milk and honey.' He repeated these words with assurance, yet they stirred restlessly and laughed at him.

'Only,' warned Caleb, 'rebel not against the Lord. . . .'

Suddenly, as I lay prone, the temper of the people changed to a viciousness we had never experienced before. There came a rushing in the air and the thud of stones as men scooped up jagged bits of rock and hurled them at us. Stoning their captains, their priest and their prophet.

XXIV

These Our Saplings

Just as suddenly as it had started, the ugly mood was over. Out of
compunction? I could not tell. Only that the great, childlike mass
of ungovernable people hesitated, and I, inevitably, interceded,
picking myself up and making myself ready to propitiate.

The Voice came wearily and, in the silence which then shut
down, I could hear the last stones rattling to the ground as
clenched fists opened.

'How long will this people despise me?' inquired the Lord,
bleakly, I thought, as if deprived of authority: even, it would
seem, a diminished God, sapped by the intransigence of his
chosen, his resolution now yielding to their contrary purposes. I
looked about me. Deprived? Diminished? How could that be? Or
was it I who had spoken? Perhaps not the Lord's voice, but my
own? Which of us in that moment had despaired? 'And how long
will they not believe in me, for all the signs which I have wrought
among them?' But there was a gathering of strength. 'I shall smite
them with the pestilence . . .' – my mouth echoed his words – '. . .
and disinherit them, and shall make of thee a nation greater and
mightier than they.'

Make out of whom? I surveyed the sullen host, not cowed, not
tearful, not childishly pledging yet again their so easily
reversible obedience, but stubborn, rebellious, still dangerous in
temper. Even so, I turned to the Lord, where the cloud smoked at
my side. 'Then the Egyptians shall hear it,' I reminded him, 'for
thou broughtest up this people in thy might from among them,
and they will tell it to the inhabitants of this land.' But why
should the Lord care about rumours? 'They have heard that thou,
Lord, sit in the midst of this people; for thou, Lord, art seen face
to face, and thy cloud standeth over them, and thou goest before

them, in a pillar of cloud by day, and in a pillar of fire by night.'

I paused, girding up my courage, determined to outface the Lord. Were they not still my people?

'Now if thou shalt kill this people as one man, then the nations which have heard the fame of thee will speak, saying, Because the Lord was not able to bring this people into the land which he sware unto them, therefore – therefore, he hath slain them in the wilderness.'

But had I, at last, gone too far? A testy old man, scolding his God? I noted approval in Caleb's watchfulness, yet Caleb was sometimes too forthright. I saw perplexity in Joshua's more critical gaze.

'And now, I pray thee . . .' – gently, as to a recalcitrant child rather than to the Lord God of Israel – '. . . let the power of the Lord be great, according as thou hast spoken, saying, the Lord is slow to anger. . . .'

I hastened on, for it had to be said, even as he himself had once said it. 'Pardon, I pray thee . . .' – my voice conciliatory, fearful as I was now at all that had taken place, eager with supplication, yet without much hope – '. . . pardon, I pray thee, the iniquity of this people according to the greatness of thy mercy, and according as thou hast forgiven this people, from Egypt even until now.'

A long silence, the cloud for the first time but a pale shadow across the tent and the people shuffling awkwardly, their rebellion still determined as they waited for the Lord's judgement. At last the Voice came. It was measured and indifferent, accepting my plea yet, as always, in the Lord's own ambiguous fashion: 'I have pardoned according to thy word.' This, at least, and my body began shaking with relief.

'But,' the Voice continued, 'but in very deed, as I live, and as all the earth shall be filled with the glory of the Lord; because all those men who have seen my glory, and my signs, which I wrought in Egypt and in the wilderness, yet have tempted me these ten times, and have not hearkened to my voice; surely they shall not see the land which I sware unto their fathers, neither shall any of them that despised me see it.'

Was it the wind rising? Or was it just a low sighing which ran through the host? Was it the breath of lamentation or gratitude?

'Say unto them,' the Voice directed me, 'your carcases shall fall in this wilderness. . . .'

This at least I had expected. We were to remain here, a people of the wilderness, going no farther until the disobedient generation had died out. They would die in this desert, at Kadesh, but naturally, each in his own time. Not every one together, blotted out by the Lord's pestilence.

'And all that were numbered of you, according to your whole number, from twenty years old and upward, which have murmured against me.'

This, too, had somehow to be accepted. But with grace? Could I manage grace? I thought not. For had I not brought them out of Egypt, in the face of their continual disobedience, shifting and inconstant as the sands we trod? I considered, rebelliously, that I had perhaps been called upon to endure rather more than the Lord. And now, was it all to be lost?

'They shall surely die in the wilderness.' The Voice was implacable. 'Save Caleb the son of Jephunnah, and Joshua the son of Nun.'

I heard the two caught breaths beside me, and saw the two stumbling movements as Caleb and Joshua fell before the Lord.

'My servant Caleb, because he hath another spirit with him, and hath followed me fully, him shall I bring into the land whereinto he went; and his seed shall possess it. To him shall I give the land that he hath trodden upon, and to his children, because he hath wholly followed the Lord.'

I watched Caleb as the tears flowed over his scarred face into his red-gold beard.

'Joshua the son of Nun, who standeth before thee . . .' – now Joshua was prostrate before the Lord – '. . . he shall go in thither: encourage thou him; for he shall cause Israel to inherit it.'

There was warning in this, though I doubted that the people understood it as such.

'But your little ones,' and the Voice softened, 'which ye said should be a prey, and your children, which this day have no knowledge of good and evil, they shall go in thither; them will I bring in, and they shall know the land which ye have rejected; and unto them shall I give it, and they shall possess it.'

The children shall know the land. I knelt down, repentant of my unruliness and grieving for my people who had borne, however discordantly, the heat and burden of the long day, and now were judged to be unworthy. But at least something would be saved out of this defeat and our journey vindicated by a sturdier, more pliant generation. These our saplings, fresh to inherit the promises of the Lord.

'And your children . . .' – the Voice sharpened, lest we become complacent – '. . . shall be wanderers in the wilderness forty years; and shall bear your whoredoms until your carcases be consumed in the wilderness.'

The Voice had still not finished.

'After the number of the day in which ye spied out the land, even forty days, for every day a year, shall ye bear your iniquities, even forty years.'

Then the Lord added the words that chilled my heart, though the people were indifferent and gave but scant attention: 'And ye shall know my alienation.'

Could there be any other sorrow? The Lord withdrawn. His presence in our midst but no longer compassionate. Waiting forty years which, in his sight, would be but the passing of a moment. While my people were imprisoned in the desert, living, suffering, loving a little, and, ultimately, dying. Yet, they had sinned. . . . They had rejected, utterly, the Promised Land.

The men who had brought back evil reports died strangely. And of course the people repented, as they always did, mourning their stupidity and lightly promising amendment. 'Lo,' they said, 'we be here, and shall go up unto the place which the Lord hath promised: for we have sinned.'

So I rebuked them, though pitying their silly sorrow. 'Wherefore now do ye transgress the commandments of the Lord, seeing it shall not prosper? Go not up, for the Lord is not among you: that ye be not smitten down before your enemies.'

But they persisted, even though the ark of the covenant did not depart out of the camp. I also did not go, nor did Aaron, or Caleb, or Joshua, or many of those who began to understand the unwisdom of defying the Lord, with whatever good intention.

As for those who went, the Amalekites descended upon them and destroyed them.

--- XXV ---

The Rod in Flower

We settled down. Strange, that within a short time, it was as if this double rejection – that of the Promised Land by my people and that of my people by the Lord – had worked a reconciliation. The Lord still talked with me from the mercy seat. Aaron and Eleazar still served him assiduously at the altar. The cloud of smoke and fire still brooded over the tent of meeting. My people, knowing they had now a place of belonging, took care to instruct their children in the Lord's commandments, and the children were fearless and eager to serve.

We became a people rather different from what had been intended. Still chosen, but in a different way and for a different purpose. No longer straining into a precarious future, we became the guardians of that future, holding it within our hands, shaping it according to the Lord's will, and knowing that, eventually, it would take wing and leave this place, confidently to enter its inheritance.

In this new way of life, my people became nomad shepherds and cattle-herders, roaming the wilderness of Zin but returning always to where the blue and purple and scarlet of the tent of meeting beckoned from our main encampment at Kadesh. Discipline was stern, yet, curiously, the people were seldom disobedient – perhaps because, in a complicated way, their life was now secure. Kadesh was home. This was no Promised Land. There was no glory and, therefore, there were no hazards. The sheep and cattle flourished and the labour made few demands. Life for the Israelite man and woman became now a matter of looking to their own comfort, of acquiring goods, of establishing settled dwellings. Seeing all this, I decided it was probably the most that could have been expected of a slave people, bred through centuries of dependence, and incapable of grasping the suffering and the ecstasy of following the Lord into a strange land.

The children, thanks to Eleazar and his young Levitic teachers, grew apart from their parents, a flock of zealots, avidly dedicated to the Lord's commands.

It was indeed a better outcome than I could have dared to predict.

There were, inevitably, the occasional outbursts of revolt. Notably in yet another, final, dispute over leadership. Again, this trouble arose among our own family, where my authority and that of Aaron were challenged by the Levite Korah, aided secretly by Dathan and Abiram of the tribe of Reuben. I discovered that Korah had gathered two hundred and fifty of his own men in order to confront Aaron and myself. Did he then feel so insecure? Yet he was casual in his defiance. 'Ye take too much upon you,' he said airily, flapping his hand at me in dismissal, then making his unanswerable accusation. 'Seeing all the congregation are holy, every one of them, and the Lord is among them: wherefore then lift ye up yourselves above the assembly of the Lord?'

This was Miriam again. Also, they had no logic. Always, I was to be their holiness, freeing them of its undoubted inconveniences. But every now and then the people suddenly remembered their holiness, which suited their desire for a little easy power. I bowed my head before this new assault, seeing the inevitable result and surprised that they did not. Was I always to be vindicated at the expense of blood and death? I was aware, springing from deep within me, of a vast, new, uncontrollable impatience with this endlessly rebellious people.

'In the morning,' I told them, matching their revolt with my own, 'the Lord will show who are his, and who is holy.'

But what is it to be holy? And who would wish it upon himself?

'This do,' I said. 'Take you censers, Korah, and all your company; and put fire therein, and put incense upon them before the Lord tomorrow: and it shall be that the man whom the Lord doth choose, he shall be holy. . . .'

I was silent, regarding them with pity and disgust. 'Ye take too much upon you, ye sons of Levi,' I added softly, and perhaps my use of their own words was the more effective for being so quiet, for they shifted uneasily, not knowing how to deal with this ageing man, who looked so ineffectual and unresisting.

But something more was needed, and I made the necessary effort to bring them to their senses.

'Seemeth it but a small thing unto you, that the God of Israel hath separated you from the congregation of Israel, to bring you near to himself; to do the service of the tabernacle of the Lord, and to stand before the congregation to minister unto them; and that he hath brought thee near, and all thy brethren the sons of Levi with thee?'

I added, with a rap of my old, caustic tongue: 'And seek ye the priesthood also?'

Yes, the spasm on Korah's face told me as much.

'Therefore, thou and all thy company are gathered together against the Lord,' I pointed out. Then, probing: 'And Aaron, what is he that ye murmur against him?'

I sent for Dathan and Abiram, but they would not come, so I went out to them.

'We shall not come up,' they said. 'Is it a small thing that thou hast brought us up out of a land flowing with milk and honey . . .' – was Egypt now a precious memory? – '. . . to kill us in the wilderness, but that thou must need make thyself also a prince over us?'

Ah, yes. I winced. Even after all the years.

'Moreover,' they pressed me, 'thou hast not brought us into a land flowing with milk and honey, nor given us inheritance of fields and vineyards.' Then, perhaps remembering the Lord's generally wrathful protection of his prophet, and perhaps beginning to wish they had not joined so eagerly with Korah and his company: 'Wilt thou put out the eyes of these men? We shall not come up.'

I grew angry at that, and complained bitterly to the Lord. Had I hurt one of them? Would I, their prophet, afflict them? But the next day, Korah assembled his men complacently at the door of the tent of meeting and, seeing this, I feared for them. Was this not a dangerous test that I had set, offering up incense for such an unholy purpose? Was it their fault, these foolish men, if they had forgotten Nadab and Abihu? I had not forgotten. Yet I had devised the test. And I had not warned them. I trembled, knowing there could be only one end to their temerity, and, hastily, Aaron and I reminded the Lord of his promises. 'O God,' we prayed, falling upon our faces in defence of this troublesome company and their innocent families, 'O God, the God of the spirits of all flesh, shall one man sin, and wilt thou be wroth with all the congregation?'

But the Lord would not listen, and the families, who after all had done no wrong, were separated out in a place apart. And there I spoke to them for the last time, still in my strange mood of violence invited.

'Hereby ye shall know that the Lord hath sent me to do all these works; for I have not done them of mine own mind.'

(But was that true? Did my mind not enter in, shaping a portion of the Lord's will towards them?)

'If these men', I told the people, 'die the common death of all men, or if they be visited after the visitation of all men, then the Lord hath not sent me. But if the Lord make a new thing, and the ground open her mouth, and swallow them up, with all that appertain to them, and they go down alive into the pit; then ye shall understand that these men have despised the Lord.'

My terms, not the Lord's. For a moment my tongue seemed to betray me. For was this not an evil thing that I did, standing now in the Lord's place, no longer an intermediary but stating my own requirements, the Lord being constrained to manifest his pleasure or displeasure under my direction? But I shut my mind against doubt, no longer heeding the cost, and perhaps, just a little, desiring this vengeance though I had prayed against it. Indeed, in its sudden dreadfulness, it seemed an unnecessary ending: the ground parting, so that Korah and Dathan and Abiram and all their companions and all their families were buried, going alive into the pit, and the men who had offered incense being destroyed utterly in the fire.

Watching as the earth opened, I shuddered. Not at their going, but at my own arrogance. Knowing that the Lord had complied with my will. Not out of his own anger, but because I had said it would be so. What had I done? I stared at the black crumpling of the piled rocks, the lips of the pit now smoothly closing. Soon no wrinkle would be seen on the desert's surface. I tried to tell myself that this destruction was as I had always thought such things to be – a natural catastrophe, an unsuspected movement of the earth's crust, erupting just at this moment, just in this place. Nothing to do with me. Yet, as I knew, evil had been called up. I was no longer in possession of myself; the dark had been let in and was taking over. Had not Korah been right? 'Ye take too much upon you,' he had said. And for that he had died.

Afterwards we took the censers, because they were holy even if the men who had used them were unholy, and we scattered the fire and beat the censers into a covering for the altar and we made a memorial that only the seed of Aaron should burn incense before the Lord.

But the next day the people were murmuring against me, saying that Aaron and I had between us killed the people of the Lord. At this I quailed, my queer madness a little spent, anxious only to avert the Lord's fresh kindling against the malcontents, and hearing with growing fear his threats of pestilence. 'Take thy censer,' I cried to Aaron, 'and put fire therein from off the altar, and lay incense thereon, and carry it quickly unto the congregation, and make atonement for them: for there is wrath gone out from the Lord.' I looked about me, appalled by what I saw. 'Carry it quickly. The plague is begun.'

I watched him go, my elder brother, that selfish, scheming, boastful priest, as he ran – yes indeed, he ran – to save his people. Careless now of pride, he went swiftly into the midst of them, seeing that the plague was already rife, and hastily offering his ritual prayers even as those around him were struck down.

And I? In that moment, there was no virtue in me. I stood there bound, the net of my offences shackling me.

But I watched how Aaron turned valiantly to raise up the necessary atonement. I saw in him a new and humble dignity, as he stood between the dead and the living – the High Priest of the Lord God of Israel, now a frightened man but shielding his people with the incontrovertible barrier of his own sanctity. For did he not bear upon his forehead the holiness of the Lord?

So the plague was stayed, and Aaron returned to me, the fear wet upon his brow. Yet, as I looked, I saw the words written there – *Holy to the Lord* – shining unclouded through the dust and sweat, even as upon the crown of gold at his anointing. But these words were red like wounds, and I knelt before him, having learned at last to reverence my brother.

There was a sequel to this, for I saw the need to reinforce Aaron's authority. I took from each of the twelve houses of our people a stave, upon which was written the name of the house. And I took also Aaron's rod, on which his own name was written. These I laid in the tabernacle before the Lord, telling the people that the Lord would choose the man whose rod should bud, and that then the murmuring must cease. This I also did because I mourned for Korah and his grasping company, and saw a way to make some kind of reparation, granting him, though dead, a milder test than that to which he had so rashly consented.

The next morning I went to the tent of meeting and brought out the rods, holding them on high before the people, then handing each to its rightful owner. All of them were black and stained and scarred with much usage, as they had always been. But the rod of Aaron had budded in the night, and now it put forth blossom and bore ripe almonds. It was a thing of wonder, and the people gasped to see it.

I lifted the rod in all its tender beauty, then placed it within the tabernacle to be a living witness to Aaron's choosing.

Was it magic? I could not tell. I recalled my earlier rejection of such marvels, yet now, observing the pale flowers – petals that I could touch, with a bloom still upon them – I felt that the magic, if such it were, had been justified.

However, there were still the voices of discontent; the people avoided the priests and looked at them sullenly.

'Behold, we perish, we are undone . . .'

'. . . we are all undone.'

They gathered in small groups, nodding together, casting frightened glances at the tent of meeting.

'Every one that cometh near . . .'

'. . . that cometh near unto the tabernacle of the Lord. . . .'

A hush, and then the word was spoken:

'. . . dieth.'

Grey faces, sweating and showing fear, and meeting the fear with despondency.

'Shall we perish, all of us?'

Only a few whispers, but I knew they must not grow. And certainly the deaths of Korah and his people had been a terrible thing. So we ordered, as once we had done before, that the children of Israel should no longer come near the tent of meeting, not being strong enough to encounter its holiness. The Levites only, and they treading delicately, were to do the service of the Lord, and no stranger might approach.

I understood then something of the meaning of those earlier words of the Lord, spoken on Mount Horeb, so incomprehensible to me at the time: '. . . and Aaron', the Lord had said, 'shall bear the iniquity of the holy things'.

It occurred to me now that holiness was neither sweet nor lovely, that my people might admire it. Nor was it homely and comfortable. Rather, it was power, naked and terrible. And those who handled it must be circumspect lest they provoke their own deaths, or the deaths of others. A man could encompass much mischief. As I had done.

I thought about Aaron, standing in such resolute fear between the dead and the living, and I knew that even I might not have dared so to confront the Lord. Yet he had done so, and had prevailed, his rod acknowledging his grace and breaking into flower.

---- XXVI ----

The Waters of Meribah

If Aaron had retained holiness, I had lost it. Something had departed from me, and what was left turned to a sickness, squeezing me dry. I was like a once-green tree built to withstand the desert deprivations but now a husk, the core of it powdered into soft decay.

During these days, gentleness finally drained out of me, as if, in their new contentment, my people had acquired it in exchange for their own earlier truculence. All their fractious mutinies seemed now to lodge within me: they became docile with my docility, reasonable with my reasonableness, diligent with my diligence. While I? I hugged their old resentments, nourished their disobedience. So we changed places, their past rebellions becoming my present ones, and with them a black despair that opened like a pit before me, closing its mouth and swallowing me as the earth had opened to swallow Korah.

I no longer knew myself. Nor did I know the Lord; I was withdrawn from his presence as he was from mine. Presumably I must have borne myself much as usual, and if I held back from conversation, maybe my people attributed it to my years; even, ironically, to an increase in holiness, which tended to separate me from lesser clay. Or perhaps they saw me as just a sad old man who had lost the comfort of the young, dark body that had lain so sweetly against his.

I remained indifferent to their thoughts, nursing my sickness, and nursing my visions. For the visions now came thick and fast, but no longer bringing reassurance. I was open to darkness and without defences. Never did I encounter that sober congregation reading the law before my tablets, nor the woman of the house blessing the Sabbath light. No, the visions reverted to the fearful desolation of that first sending when, as an officious young prince, I had seen the walls of Moloch rising where our Hebrew builders worked in the Egyptian sun.

Not that my present visions were so clearly defined. They came in a jumble of unrelated blood and terror. I would sit by one of the pools of Kadesh, distanced from my people and gazing into the waters, dreading what I must see, and panting to escape, yet with a part of me relishing the fearfulness.

There were cold, strange wastes of land, white-covered with crystalline stuff, men and women lying blackened, yet red with blood, upon the white. There was a deep well, dried up, and my living people crammed down its gaping throat, with stone slabs placed neatly on top. There were dark rooms, the windows barred, and women cowering as the stout doors failed to resist the howling mob. There was a tower upon a hill, and the horde breaking in, and a priest – was he a priest? – who went deliberately among his people, cutting their throats one by one and then his own, before the horde could reach them. There was a dark ravine, brimming with bare corpses, and a few soldiers toppling other naked but yet living bodies on to those who already lay there, dead. There was singing. Oh yes, there was singing. Serious faces bent over their music-making. The sound of jubilation. Though it was no matter for rejoicing, even if their gaolers sat much moved and often with the tears of musical appreciation falling on to their uniforms.

And there was another patch of yard between high buildings, this time with row upon row of tattered figures standing barefoot in what seemed a terrible cold. But other men, warmly clad, came forward eagerly, pouring water over these people out of long tubes, so that in only a few moments each figure grew stiff. I watched as one of the gaolers then went up and snapped off a man's arm, laughing and waving it at his fellows, and laying it with a hideous courtesy at the owner's immobile feet.

I could not halt the seeing. Vision piled on vision, and always of my people suffering and dying. Was this their future? Was there to be no end to it? I would crouch over the waters of the great oasis, weighing up the dark and the light, yet finding only darkness, a world constructed upon the pillars of Sheol by those who did not care. And my people consumed.

But if in my body I cowered beside the pool of Kadesh, yet also I was there in the ravine, under layer upon layer of the dead. I ran weeping to gather up the snapped-off arms, striving impossibly to join them back to those cold pillars that had once been men. I waited patiently, in the last moments, as the merciful leader of that small flock let out each life cleanly, taking my own turn to escape the hands of our tormentors. I floated insubstantially, among those who had become but wisps of smoke upon the fetid air.

Crouching there, I struggled to say the words of consolation. Could any man do this thing? No man, surely, out of his own pity. . . . Possibly, out of his own dereliction. The eternal God is thy dwelling-place, I told those other victims, striving to lift them up into the Lord's compassion, to lay them in his everlasting arms. But this I could not do. For indeed, they were already there, and the arms were beneath them. Afterwards, each time, I knew that I had also done these things out of my own need.

I knew there had to be an ending to the sickness, but I was helpless to precipitate it. I remembered that after the wickedness of the golden calf, it had seemed as if a sore had burst open in my people; they were suddenly free of uncleanness. Perhaps I needed some such release, some necessary explosion.

Perhaps, too, I argued, it was not so unnatural, this present dark. Surely a man cannot become the vessel of God and always retain holiness? Surely the vessel is not built to withstand the fire poured in? Had I not feared this very danger, as I knelt before the burning bush? There might well be flaws in this vessel, now cracked open and crumbling. I sought to comfort myself with such ideas, but there was no comfort; only a stirring of panic, as if I approached some moment from which I might not return.

The moment came when our springs ran dry and there was no water for the people. Although it was a serious matter, I did not doubt it would right itself; it was merely a passing drought against which the families should have been prepared. I listened to their complaints with growing irritation. Again the cries: would God we had died when our brethren died! Again the recriminations: why have ye brought us into this wilderness, that we should die here, we and our cattle? This time there was an added jibe: it is no place of figs, or vines, or pomegranates . . . and the ultimate and sobering reminder, 'Neither is there any water to drink.'

Aaron and I besought the Lord to aid us and indeed he answered with a few simple instructions. I was to take my rod – that staff which had parted the Sea of Reeds – and assemble the people, speaking to the rocks whence the dried spring had issued.

'So,' explained the Lord, 'thou shalt give the congregation and their cattle to drink.'

The people were still grumbling as I carried the rod out of the tent of meeting and gathered the whole company before the rocky hillside. Had I not mediated many times on their behalf, and had it not always ended in their favour? Did not the Lord's mercy drop down upon this people through the channel of my own tenderness?

But I had no tenderness. As I looked at the dried-up watercourse where now no moisture trickled and where the great rock basins stood with their small residue of gritty water, with scum floating and a rising smell of decay, I asked myself, was not their fear justified? As I stared out across the silent, shuffling host it was through a red haze of anger. How long must I be afflicted with this contumacious people? It was I, not the Lord, who said these words. Was I taking upon myself his suffering? Furious with guilt, I turned on my people. 'Hear now, ye rebels,' I taunted them, the desert wavering in the tide of blood that blocked my sight, 'shall we bring you forth water out of this rock?'

We. No more the Lord pouring out his manna and his quails and his springs of water to console his frightened children. I would do this thing out of my own power. Not speaking to the rocks in the Lord's name as I had been bidden. Well, were not many of us skilled in divining the sources of hidden springs? A desert-living people become easily aware of how the wilderness is formed and where its treasures lie couched, ready to be tapped by their cunning from out of the dry soil. I, not the Lord, would therefore do this thing. But not in love, not in humility, not on my knees before the Lord, his vessel, the channel of his gift. The vessel was broken, and the light I had borne turned to ashes.

In that moment Aaron, whose face was blanched white even in the strong sunlight, knew what I was about, for he shrank from me, backing away as I lifted my hand and smote the rock with my rod. Still in the reddened mist of fury, still choked with the ashes of my holiness. I struck the rock twice. Not from any urge

— 160 —

towards emphasis but to assert that there were now two powers actively at work among my people.

At first, all was still and dry and silent, then, ignoring my motive, the spring was obedient. It came abundantly, plashing over the rocks and down into the filthy pools, washing everything clean. It sparkled gaily, tumbling ever faster until it became a rushing stream, eventually filling our deep rock basins until they lay dark and brimming and placid.

I stumbled past Aaron, who was still shrinking from me, past my silently dispersing people, past a Joshua who stood looking at me with appalled disbelief. I climbed up out of the place, having refused the required invocation to the Lord and vouchsafing no blessing for his gift.

The way was barren and deserted, twisting along the hot flanks of a steeply gullied hill. The water from a dozen cool freshets now pattered among the rocks, seeking the floor of the desert, and as I climbed I remembered the dry watercourse of Horeb up which I had travelled to meet the Lord.

Now I would meet him once again, to learn his judgement. So I thrust myself along a narrow cleft, coming out at last to a level place, where I threw myself to the ground, crawling into the darkness of shadowed stone and resting my burning forehead against its damp smoothness.

'The Lord shall smite thee with madness . . .' – was this my own voice, or was it out of the stone, out of the waters? – '. . . with madness, and with blindness, and with astonishment: and thou shalt grope at noonday, as the blind gropeth in darkness. . . .'

Then there was silence, save for the continual murmur of the water as it trickled down the hillside. I listened to it, lying there hour by hour, emptied of thought and feeling, waiting for the Lord's wrath to light upon me. I lay as if already dead, beyond repentance, beyond expectation, my body tenantless, my spirit void. Nothing left but a vast hole where my rebellion had been.

Yet no destroying vengeance came. Instead, the sound of the waters grew into a tumult, so that nothing else existed and I was blind and deaf and dumb. The dry hillside, the stones, the noonday sun – all these had gone from my sight. There remained only the water, crushing, subduing, bruising. No place, no people, no journey. Only the water. Out of which came the Voice.

'See,' It murmured, 'I have set before thee this day life and good, and death and evil.'

But which had I chosen? I lay there no longer conscious of living or not living, yet aware that, totally without volition, I was making a choice. For was it not built into me, structured out of the desert, as I knelt before the burning bush, walked beside the pillar of cloud and, shielded by its fire by night, listened to the Lord's voice as I stood in the bowl of light upon Mount Horeb, watched before the golden wings of the cherubim in the blue and purple and scarlet of his tent of meeting?

My choice. And suddenly, I knew astonishment – the astonishment of hope. I could no longer see the spring, but that was because now it rose within me, sluicing away the blackened places, rinsing out the madness, dissipating my wickedness in a thousand droplets of light. The water of expiation.

Out of the water there came a new innocence. I was lapped by it, the spring rising ever higher and bursting from me in cascades of sound, so that I felt myself to be swaddled within it, no longer the swaddling of a fear which had touched me long ago, but now the cradle of safe keeping. The waters rose and rose, now filling the universe. I was aware of the universe. I lay within it, and the universe lay within me.

'See now', said the Voice, 'that I, even I, am he, and there is no God with me. I kill, and I make alive; I have wounded, and I heal: and there is none that can deliver out of my hand.'

The cup restored. The light safely housed.

I remained there all day. Later I found food placed at a distance and knew that Joshua must have been near. But I touched nothing, even as I had touched no food upon Mount Horeb.

At last, lifting myself to my feet, though slowly and with infinite stiffness and with my bones creaking in their joints, I looked about me. Meribah, I told myself. This place shall be known for ever by that name. Meribah – the waters of contention. But not, as my people would later imagine, their contention. No, the contention had been mine. There was also another name: Massah – the testing. This too belonged to the place. Again, not my people's testing, but my own. I had failed in that testing, even as they had so often failed. Yet, and this seemed strange and wonderful, instead of striking me down in that moment, the Lord had permitted me to work his will. Even more strange, the waters I had invoked in such anger had brought reconciliation. I had come back into myself, although I might fail again and the cost was going to be one which I would not wish to pay.

'Because ye believed not in me . . .' – the Lord's voice, making it plain – '. . . to sanctify me in the eyes of the children of Israel, therefore ye shall not bring this assembly into the land which I have given them.'

This then was to be the price. A hard price, to relinquish the cherished reward. But also a just price – and the Lord had been merciful.

So I knelt in the place of Meribah and took the price upon me.

The Words

Miriam died at Kadesh after some years of seclusion. As far as possible she kept away from me in those latter days – also, curiously, from Aaron, who was grieved by what he saw as a wilful alienation. Apart from her serving-women, almost the only people she permitted near her were Gershom and Eliezer. They visited her devotedly, behaving as if she were mother in place of Zipporah, and displaying towards her a loving delicacy of attention I should not have thought possible in those two cold men.

Catching sight of her now and then, I saw her stooped and slow of pace, head bowed and veiled, her abundant hair cropped close. She spoke seldom, and I was reminded, with a shock of dreadful pity, of my silent Cushite woman. Incredulous, I began to realise that the silence of both was the silence of peace. Miriam no longer dominated, no longer danced her barbaric dances, no longer sang her triumph songs of battle, but nor did she scheme or jostle for power. At first, I thought her – seeing her so bent – as a strong tool now broken and unusable. Yet this was not so, for she was in no way broken, only come to an unexpected tranquillity.

Her earlier reputation as a soothsayer still followed her, though she no longer forecast the future, spending much of her time in search of herbs, from which she made up simple medicines. But always alone, save when either Gershom or Eliezer went to lead her back – confiding, even childlike – to the safety of the camp.

Her death came quietly, and the women mourned her, for to them she remained a magical figure, even more impressive during the years of her withdrawal than in her fierceness and pride. Aaron was much shaken by her going. He was nearer to her in age and closer in affection than I had ever been.

And I? Yes, I mourned her also in the tightness of my heart. For though I could not call up love, I remembered that it was the child Miriam who had waited so impatiently near that basket in the reeds, and that had it not been for her tenacity I should never have known the blinding Egyptian sun which was to shine upon me so propitiously that day. So I was grateful, though I took little part in the ritual of mourning. This was noticed, and Gershom and Eliezer both looked on me with contempt. But did they understand, I wondered, what Miriam had been? And did they understand that, although I had long since lost my bitterness against her, she had been dead to me from the day my Cushite wife had forsaken my tent?

One by one they dropped away, the older generation. Their sons and daughters replaced them; sturdier folk, bred in freedom. Kadesh – that dusty encampment – was gradually transformed by many stone-built dwellings and twisting alleyways, yet never too thoroughly contrived because we knew we must not, in this place, set our hearts on permanence. Though when the time came, we had some difficulty in leaving Kadesh, since the Edomite people refused us passage through their land.

'Let us pass, I pray thee,' I asked, then promising, 'we shall not pass through field or vineyard, neither shall we drink of the water of the wells: we shall go along the king's high way, we shall not turn aside to the right hand nor to the left, until we have passed thy border.'

But still they refused, threatening to come out against us with the sword. So I appealed to their cupidity: 'If we drink of thy water, I and my cattle, then shall I give the price thereof.'

Again we were refused, the Edomites stirring like a swarm of angry bees. So we turned aside, making the longer journey which brought us, soon after leaving Kadesh, to the foot of Mount Hor. We rested there, intending to stay only a few days, but now I watched Aaron constantly, knowing it would not be long before he was taken from us, and that it was a blessing we were not half-way into the kingdom of the uncharitable Edomites.

He was increasingly fragile, my brother, and Eleazar had taken over all his duties. He must have known he was facing his death, though he did not speak of it, merely sitting at the door of his tent, his head shaking uncontrollably, his eyes focused on some interior consideration, cloudy and more faded than they had been, his hands trembling restlessly in his great age, as he picked at his garments, never still.

I was a good few years behind him. And now, and during the months of our journey from Kadesh towards the Promised Land, I was aware that I remained strong; able, with an upraised finger, to hold the people obedient. They were resolute and unafraid, these younger men, lean and hard and desert-skilled, sharp-eyed in their wary defiance of the outer tribes, and bonded into one great host, now fully steeped in the Lord's commandments.

Seeing their readiness to obey me, even though as individuals they were a self-willed and passionate people, I would remember, with ironic appraisal, the unruly days of the exodus from Egypt. These were the Lord's new chosen, made possible by their vacillating, unsatisfactory, yet always tenderly remembered forerunners. I rejoiced over these young men, seeing them as worthy of being chosen.

But indeed, they too would often fail. Were they not human? When we left the shelter of Kadesh behind us and they were exposed to the pressure of pagan beliefs, then they would fail, and even forget their heritage. I could see a time, perhaps many times, when the Lord's commandments would become but a blurred memory of some other, abandoned age, fragments of which would still hold a superstitious awe.

Because of this, I decided to leave the people something more substantial than my remembered teaching. There would be priests and sons of priests, and again sons and sons of priests, and the word of the Lord would travel down the centuries. But in the telling it could become distorted. Therefore I must make a record which would not be open to misinterpretation, but which, after their many and often disastrous stumblings, would be there to call my people back. The pure spring of the Lord's holiness.

So, with the help of scribes, I began my work. The Words: this was the name by which the book would come to be known. The repetition of the law. I felt satisfied by this. There would be those in the future who would learn from my book. It would even be discovered – this I saw, in a moment of exaltation – having been lost, and hidden, then found again in a time of great need, and a king would use it to recall the people of Israel to their proper worship of the Lord. The book. The Words. Bearing the breath of God.

I worked furiously, an unwonted task, shut within my tent and toiling to set it all down: that long story of our life since Horeb, the reassertion of the Lord's Ten Commandments, the revelation of his law, and the Lord's great promise of the Land. 'For,' I wrote, 'ask now of the days that are past, which were before thee, since the day that God created man upon the earth, and from the one end of heaven unto the other, whether there hath been any such thing as this great thing is, or hath been heard like it?' Then, knowing how easily words may be twisted: 'Ye shall not add unto the word which I command you, neither shall ye diminish from it, that ye may keep the commandments of the Lord your God which I command you. Only . . .' – mistrustfully – '. . . take heed to thyself, and keep thy soul diligently, lest thou forget the things which thine eyes saw.'

But I must die in this land, I thought to myself. I must not go over the Jordan. They would go over, and, should they become disobedient, the Lord would scatter them, few in number, among the nations. Yet even so, wherever they should turn back to the Lord, there they would find him. And, in the end, after much tribulation, they would be established in their own land.

'The Lord thy God . . .' – I wrote the Words with certainty – '. . . will turn thy captivity, and have compassion upon thee, and will return' – yes – 'and gather thee from all the peoples, whither the Lord thy God hath scattered thee.'

They were the chosen, and among them, in every generation, there would be those few just men whose saving presence, bearing the burden of the world's suffering, would atone for corruption.

Day after day, enclosed in my tent, I wrote down everything that the Lord had told me, careful to omit nothing, since I could not be there to repair an omission. Ah yes, there lay the rub. 'I can no more go out and come in: and the Lord hath said unto me, Thou shalt not go over this Jordan. . . .' Impossible to omit, among all those matters which must not be omitted, my own childish need that my people should remember me: 'And I have led you forty years in the wilderness: your clothes are not waxen old upon you, and thy shoe is not waxen old upon thy foot.'

But what of my own clothes, my own shoes? Were they not used up? The clothing which is my body and the clothing which is the spirit that walked beside the Lord, were not both somewhat tattered? Beset by doubts and fears, I thought often about this seemingly endless task of mine, unfulfilled and, I reasoned, unfulfillable, because of my exclusion from the Promised Land. I even left the book of the Words unfinished, telling the scribes that they must add my final message before I died and then a description of my death. But still I fretted, seeing no proper ending and yearning for that ultimate moment when my people entered their heritage. I would walk at their head, knowing that just as I had led their fathers out of slavery, so I had led this new generation into freedom. My achievement. My rounded task. Then might I die. . . . Ah yes! Still, in age, the same obstinate prophet who had always and so persistently argued with his God.

Yet I knew it would not be like that. There would be no triumphal procession. Only a weary fighting to establish this Promised Land about us, a putting on of its hills and valleys as a garment which, once worn, would never be discarded. While I, forbidden by the Lord, would remain here, in the wilderness – the chosen victim, bearing my people's ancient, troubled face.

At night, the scribes away in their own tents, I would open my mind to the precious fragments that the Lord had carved upon my bones and poured into my blood. And it was on one of these occasions, when I saw the lamp-wick spluttering as it burned low in its bowl, that I looked up, thinking of nothing more than whether I should fetch some oil. Darkness had gathered in the corners of the tent, and as I raised my head I saw, half shadowed, a stranger watching me. He stood quite calmly, more immediate than the young man whose gaze had attracted me in that other time, as he and his companions read from their books beneath my tablets of the law. That man had only, perhaps idly, pondered the many centuries that lay between us. This man, nearer to me in time – though this was not the reason – saw me clearly, was there beside me, even as the wild prophet had seen me before the altar of sacrifice. But the prophet had been filled with a fierce

— 168 —

reproach, whereas this man, facing me with such composure, appeared thoughtful, even compassionate.

Presently he spoke, deliberately, as if he understood my predicament and had come to teach me. I listened to his voice, which made no sound in the quiet tent, but only, in my mind, a light singsong of tones which were a little nasal and perhaps a little harsh.

'It is not thy duty', he told me, 'to complete the work. . . .'

I bowed my head, trying then to kneel to him. Yet it seemed, in his wisdom, that he would not have me kneel, acknowledging himself, if proudly, as of less account in the Lord's scale of reckoning and, while proffering humility, yet inexorably completing his message.

'But neither', he continued, 'art thou free to desist from it.'

I stared at him with a passionate intensity, knowing that, if only I could, I would wrest from him all his wisdom. I longed to hold him near, this man with the large, soft brown eyes and the somewhat haughty manner, who perhaps could share with me the secrets of how to live. But my very eagerness drove him from me, shutting out the barrier of my fleshly presence, so that, as the lamp wavered again and died, he was gone from me, gone into the shadows of another time, and I was left alone.

I clung to his words, an answer to my questioning, as if the unsatisfactory ambiguities of this long exodus had been lifted from me. Everything all at once appeared possible, even manageable. It might not stay that way, but I knew it was the answer I sought and that it was indeed the answer for all men.

I stood in the darkened tent, reaching for the other lamp and allowing myself a wry smile at the endless persistence of my awkward foolishnesses. It had taken long enough to learn the wisdom of those few words. A whole lifetime, fighting against my shadow-self. But now in this moment (perhaps only for this moment?) I had been set free. Even though, as he had told me, neither was I free. There was not, any longer, a discrepancy.

—— XXVIII ——

The Brazen Serpent

On the following day the Lord spoke to me as I sat with Aaron. He did not cloak his words. But then he never did.

'Aaron', we were told, 'shall be gathered unto his people: for he shall not enter into the land which I have given unto the children of Israel, because ye rebelled against my word at the waters of Meribah.'

It had been my rebellion, not his, yet now I could accept that we had both been involved and that Aaron, though horrified, had not prevented me.

'Take Aaron and Eleazar his son,' the Lord continued, 'and bring them up unto Mount Hor: and strip Aaron of his garments, and put them on Eleazar his son: and Aaron shall be gathered unto his people, and shall die there.'

Aaron smiled sweetly at this, the simple smile of age, a flicker of childlike innocence which fled over his old, worn face. But then he looked at me sharply, and I saw he was not at all confused, knowing exactly what we were about, and being ready.

So I gathered the company at the foot of Mount Hor, and we placed Aaron, dressed in the full robes of the High Priest of the Lord God of Israel, in the ceremonial litter, the curtains of which were as the tent of meeting, woven in blue and purple and scarlet and threaded through with gold. This was borne by his sons, Eleazar and Ithamar, and his grandson Phinehas, aided by Joshua. Together with some of our elders, we mounted the stony track to the summit of Mount Hor. I walked slowly at Aaron's side, yet still retained – I noted with foolish vanity – something of my old desert stride.

When we had reached the mountain's crest, humbly and with

the appropriate prayers we removed Aaron's priestly garments: his coat of chequerwork, his breastplate, his ephod and his robe, after which I placed them upon Eleazar so that he in turn became the High Priest of Israel, wearing Aaron's blue and purple and scarlet, and his decorated skirts with their coloured pomegranates and all the little tinkling bells, and bearing upon his head the crown of gold, holy to the Lord, which Aaron placed there with his own hands, frail yet standing upright and with dignity in that moment.

When this was done, Aaron, in his still beautiful voice, gave his son the blessing which the Lord had taught him:

'The Lord bless thee, and keep thee:
The Lord make his face to shine upon thee, and be gracious unto thee:
The Lord lift up his countenance upon thee, and give thee peace.'

After this, still firmly and with a grace that I had seldom seen in my brother, Aaron blessed the others standing near. He did not bless me, for that he might not do, but he came to me and put his hands on my shoulders, looking down at me from his great height with eyes that were suddenly clear and amused. Then he kissed my cheeks and we exchanged the tremulous smiles of those who might have said more, had there been time.

He walked apart from us, around the other face of Mount Hor, looking out towards the Promised Land which he, too, would never see. We sat in silence, knowing that for the rest of our days we should be without Aaron. There was a small, restless wind around our perch above the desert; no sound save the occasional cry of an eagle as it cruised about the topmost rocks of Hor. Later, when we went to attend Aaron, we found him half sitting, half lying, propped against a smooth rock-face, composed and still. He was clad in a plain white woollen shift, his head and feet uncovered, his sparse white hair fluttering in the small gusts of wind. I remembered how he had stood between the dead and the living, so I knelt to him, seeing him not as a tired old man but as he had been in the days of his glory, his beard then dark and glossy and curled, the full pride of his priesthood issuing from him. Indeed, in this moment of his ultimate infirmity, he was still a proud man, and, as he lay there in near-nakedness, there was upon him a look of royalty.

He gave us a little nod, as much as to say that now it was time, and his head fell backward as he died.

There was a cave near the summit of Mount Hor, and we laid Aaron on the floor of the cave, while his sons and grandson made the necessary ritual. Then we sealed the place with slabs of rock and went back down the mountainside. As we neared the waiting people, silent and attentive to our coming, they saw that Eleazar now wore the garments of the High Priest and they did obeisance.

But they wept. For they had loved Aaron, finding him genial and indulgent, nearer to them in their follies than I have ever been. They had delighted in his priestly dignity, venerating him as almost the last of the old ones. So they mourned him for the prescribed thirty days. They had, after all, known him all their lives.

When we moved out from the quiet shelter of Mount Hor, I felt curiously naked, peeled of my skin and vulnerable. Aaron lay behind us now, sightless in his mountain cave. Miriam, in Kadesh, remained a faint shadow on the desert sand. And behind Miriam, in an endless chain, the ever-diminishing shapes of my people reached far back into Egypt.

I had not loved Aaron, nor had I loved Miriam. Yet they were my own. Part of me, part of my experience. They alone shared my history, that familiar knowledge binding us together in a fashion which no stranger might fully comprehend. Now they were gone and I, in my old age, was left to remember all the trivial details of our exasperating kinship. We had spent the greater part of our lives together. Yet I had not known them. Perhaps I had not tried to know them.

Sitting in my tent at night, walking with Joshua and Caleb by day at the forefront of the host, I would shrug impatiently at such thoughts. Aaron and Miriam were gone. Possibly, in some other world beyond this world, some other entirely unimaginable state of existence, we might yet achieve understanding. Perhaps not.

But there were others, not belonging to the great company of my people. Far back across the wilderness, even maybe beyond Egypt and down in that hot land of the south where I had never been, my Cushite woman might still be living. She would be in her middle years, looking surely like any other woman of her people, all the rare knowledge of our time together probably half forgotten or shut away, unsuspected by those around her and only infrequently, if ever, taken out and examined. Unless – and here I would pause, often actually stopping in my tracks along the march, so that Caleb's sharp glance would seek me out to assess whether I might be faltering – unless there was also a boy. Then I would irritably shake my head. No, not a boy; a man now, dark like my Cushite wife, but possibly invested with my own hooded, melancholy gaze. And then the dust would blow up across the shimmering purple distance, and I would shake my head again to push it all behind me, seeing only Caleb and Joshua at my side.

Those two I would watch surreptitiously: Caleb, a dour and earthy man, practical in all his thoughts and dealings, unimaginately tenacious of his faith, open to no argument once his mind was settled – a plodding sort of man, and valuable beyond all others save only one. Joshua. On Joshua my glance would dwell with love. He was powerfully into his prime, but still for me that thin, brilliant-eyed child, trembling with his fervent enthusiasm, sensing the fire I carried, kneeling in the dusty lanes as I passed, dogging my footsteps. I would smile then, wiping the sweat from my desert-darkened face, my heart glad of these two faithful men.

But there was little opportunity, during this march, for dwelling on what was past. We faced an uncertain future, every step of the way having to be fought over. In recollection, the battles seemed endless, one no sooner concluded in our favour than another enemy would rise up to dispute our passage. To me, still leading my host into battle, still guiding them, the fighting was always the same: sickening and bloody, and holding, in the riddle of my fluctuating self, the danger that my disgusted reluctance might precipitate a brutality which I would not wish yet which I seemed powerless to withstand. For I licensed the killings, seeing in reality what previously

had only hovered on the edges of my vision: the eternal suffering of young children, those frail, inevitably condemned
victims.

As to the places where we fought, and the tribes we
encountered, these varied only in the advantage or disadvantage
of the battleground and the degree of hostility meted out to us.
Oh, certainly, the names differed. I remembered them as a
strange, harsh music: the Anakim, Sihon of Heshbon, Og of
Bashan at Edrei in the region of Argob, the two kings of the
Amorites, and all the cities of the plain; Gilead, Salecah, Aroer by
Arnon, the borders of the Geshurites and the Maacathites, and
then from Chinnereth to the sea of Arabah. A threatening music
which we silenced.

But of all that happened on that remorseless march, I
remembered most clearly the time of the serpents. We advanced
into a part of the land alive with many of these creatures; they
came teeming out of the earth, slithering rapidly over the sandy
soil, whipping out of the holes and crevices of the rocks and
hissing malignantly as they struck.

The people were in terror. Not only did they fear for their
lives (and indeed some of them died) but they feared, as of old,
the snare of the tempter. Ever since Eve our mother, we had
shunned the serpent, aware of its power, fascinated by its
wisdom, yet loathing it for what it had done and because it crept
upon its belly. Now, surrounded by its innumerable incarna-
tions, my people wept. More than the hosts drawn up against
us, more than the dust and heat of the journey, more than any
of the many desolations which had afflicted us, they
feared the multitude of fiery beasts which seethed about our
tents.

For a time it even seemed that our great host would turn back,
yet again, in this new generation, forsaking the Promised Land.
Certainly it was with difficulty that I quietened them, and then
only by a trick. The old magic, I thought ruefully, remembering
those creatures conjured in rivalry between Aaron and the
priests of Egypt. But none the less I went on with my magic,
constructing out of brass a huge, coiled serpent. This I placed
upon a standard, telling my people that if they would look upon
it, even if bitten, they would live.

Perhaps only a few of the snakes were actively vicious; perhaps my people's frenzy helped the poison to spread, so that some of them died more of fright than of snake-venom; perhaps the brazen serpent, evil made impotent, served to calm them. At any rate they managed at length to catch hold of themselves, threading their way among the lurking creatures without their first panic. Gradually it all died down, and we moved into another area, pleasantly innocent of this infestation.

Yet there was more to the matter than the fear lying on the surface. The serpents were not evil. They were a part of the wilderness, as I well knew, indifferent unless aroused. Therefore I made my brass counterpart with great seriousness, a fiery creature, yes, and flick-tongued, but with a sad and noble head rising benignly from its coils. I saw it as offering us the ancient wisdom of the desert, to be controlled, to be circumspect, to give place to all that shared the fastnesses. I saw it subtle, as Eve's serpent had been, cunning in its power, yet able to heal. Eternally cursed, yet bearing also its blessing.

As I looked upon what I had made, I understood that something was there of mystery. Perhaps it was the mystery of the Lord's dealing with Adam. The serpent had offered us knowledge, not wisdom. Only an immense and terrible acquisition, dazzling in its simplicity but lacking the necessary safeguard. It had turned out to be an unchecked lure, destined to lead Adam to his toil among the thorns and thistles and to the sweating need to fill himself with bread in place of the wisdom of God.

This is the sword, I thought – that flick of the serpent's double tongue – which ever drives us from the garden of God's presence, the garden in which we might yet be walking in his company. Now, we have inherited the thistles, and even when the Lord's compensatory herbs taste sweet, our ears, like the serpent's, are stopped.

Yet even so, and this I told myself with rising exultation, into the thorns and thistles has come once again the voice of the Lord God of Israel. And now we are called to unstop our ears. This, I felt, was the lesson of the little serpents which had so plagued us.

The people liked my brazen serpent. They kept it always with them. It looked out over their heads, raised beside the platform around which we held our assemblies. Its gaze, I told myself, was calm and all-seeing, wise with its own wisdom, which is not the same as the wisdom of God.

XXIX

The Apple of the Lord

Following much argument, I had ordered what the correct apportioning of the Land was to be when my people entered it, and how it was to be divided by lot between the twelve tribes. So, having come at last to the third mountain – that Nebo which was peculiarly to be my own – I entered the tent of meeting and spoke with the Lord.

'Get thee up into this mountain of Abarim,' the Voice advised me, using the word that signified the whole long range of which Nebo, or Pisgah, was but one peak, 'and behold the land which I have given unto the children of Israel.'

There was silence between us.

'And when thou hast seen it, then also shalt thou be gathered unto thy people, as Aaron thy brother was gathered. . . .'

Kneeling before the mercy seat, I could almost hear my bones rejoicing.

'Because ye rebelled against my word in the wilderness of Zin, in the strife of the congregation, to sanctify me at the waters before their eyes.'

Had I not known the penalty? Did I need to be reminded of it? Yet my thoughts, at that moment, were not with my own deprivation but with the holy people of Israel.

'Let the Lord, the God of the spirits of all flesh,' I asked of him, laying my forehead upon the ground, 'appoint a man over the congregation, which may go out before them, and which may come in before them, and which may lead them out, and which may bring them in. . . .'

I looked up, thinking that the golden cherubim looked particularly impassive. 'That the congregation of the Lord,' I added humbly, 'be not as sheep which have no shepherd.'

I waited then, my mind and soul open to the Lord, speaking silently the name which above all others I would have, yet knowing it must come not from the Lord's prophet but from the Lord himself. And he, as always, listened to my intention. Had he not known my heart from the beginning? The Voice was softened and agreeable.

'Take thee Joshua, the son of Nun, a man in whom is the spirit, and lay thy hand upon him; and set him before Eleazar the priest, and before all the congregation; and give him a charge in their sight. And thou shalt put of thine honour upon him, that all the congregation of the children of Israel may obey.'

At these words my heart seemed almost to burst apart, so great was my joy. So I stayed there, giving thanks, kneeling and trembling with the effort, until it was borne in upon me that I would not again be alone in this place. My tabernacle, which I had made. My – but I bowed my head in the old, ridiculously recurrent shame. Not mine, I whispered, never mine. Only, that I had some small part in it.

The candle-flame shone steadily, and the golden light grew huge and sustaining. Yet within its brilliance I saw nothing but the familiar treasures of this holy place – no distant figures, no sending from a time beyond time, for now I no longer needed such things. I was here, at the centre of time, all its manifestations now gathered up into the one Creator of the universe.

'For I shall proclaim the name of the Lord,' I promised, knowing I had little further opportunity but knowing also that my promise would endure as long as the earth endured.

Later, when I had lain there for a long time, only half-conscious and stretched across the ground, I heard the tinkle of small bells and thought it must be Aaron come now to receive me. But it was only Eleazar, wearing his priestly garments, stooping over me, then calling urgently.

The next day I had recovered, and I called the people together. I told them, as I had written in the book of the Words, that I could no more go out and come in, and that the Lord had said that I should not go over Jordan.

Watching them as I spoke, I could see they were somewhat

puzzled. Did they understand what was taking place? I thought not. They were so accustomed to my voice, telling them this, telling them that. They gazed up at me; I was no longer standing uplifted before them but seated carefully, my chair placed upon the wooden platform. Their faces seemed a little vacant, as if this was but one more out of the long succession of my homilies, my chidings, my thunderings. But as I spoke of Joshua, their attention turned towards him, imperceptibly gathering strength, so that what I had told them of myself was forgotten.

'The Lord thy God,' I said, as I had said so many times before, 'he will go over before thee. . . .' I drew Joshua up beside me. 'And Joshua, he shall go over before thee, as the Lord hath spoken.'

There were smiles then, and eager shouts, which grew to a long roaring as of a great sea, broken by thousands upon thousands of individual wavelets of joy. For they loved Joshua well, feeling at ease with him, approving him as a hard leader with a ready sword, yet who had about him that strange, heady, uncertain quality of ecstasy which drew men to him. I looked at him with love, and with compassion, for I knew the burden he would carry. 'Be strong,' I said to him, laying my hands upon his bare head as he knelt before me. 'Be strong and of a good courage: for thou shalt go with this people into the land which the Lord hath sworn unto their fathers to give them; and thou shalt cause them to inherit it.'

The people were swaying to and fro, as if a soft breeze had stirred them, their faces alight with their acceptance of this new leader.

'And the Lord,' I continued, watching Joshua's intent face, 'he it is who doth go before thee; he will be with thee, he will not fail thee, neither forsake thee: fear not, neither be dismayed.'

At this, Joshua wept, bending low and kissing my feet, even as I had once kissed the feet of my beloved Jethro, and with the same awareness of loss.

'Behold,' the Voice compelled me, 'thy days approach that thou must die: call Joshua, and present yourselves in the tent of meeting, that I may give him a charge.'

So I lifted him gently and, together with Eleazar, we went into the tabernacle, while the pillar of cloud which housed the presence of the Lord stood over the door of the tent and the people understood that the Lord himself had chosen Joshua as his own.

After the charge had been placed upon Joshua, I busied myself in giving my book of the Words to the Levites who attended the tent of meeting. 'Take this book of the law,' I ordered them, 'and put it by the side of the ark of the covenant of the Lord your God, that it may be there for a witness against thee.'

They looked at me uncertainly, making no move to obey, sullen and a little proud. So I reminded them, not with the Lord's anger but with my own.

'For I know thy rebellion, and thy stiff neck: behold, while I am yet alive with you this day, ye have been rebellious against the Lord; and how much more after my death?'

Perhaps I was disconcerted, seeing my authority now vested in another man, noting the consequent indifference of the priests. Yet there was only one prophet. I alone. I know I blustered, using my tongue as the whip it had often needed to be. Perhaps I thought to hold on to my dwindling power.

'Assemble unto me,' I commanded, 'all the elders of your tribes, and your officers, that I may speak these words in their ears, and call heaven and earth to witness against them. For I know . . .' – I was working myself up into a passion, and regretting it, yet seeing, even in my jealous anger, that it was necessary – '. . . for I know that after my death ye will utterly corrupt yourselves, and turn aside from the way which I have commanded you; and evil will befall you in the latter days; because ye will do that which is evil in the sight of the Lord, to provoke him to anger through the work of your hands.'

At this they quailed, and I knew a moment of exhilaration. The modest goat, their victim, still able to use its horns, butting them into submission with its old, accustomed wrath. I relished this, looking on their guilty faces as upon so many others who also had been truculent and wilful and perhaps, sometimes, a little contemptuous.

But then I softened, in the face of their youth and inexperience and natural pride, yet glad that I had written down the

Words, since they would surely be needed. Still an obstinate people, recalcitrant as their fathers before them. And I also. Yes, I also.

I spoke to the whole assembly, and it seemed as if, in my exaltation, those last admonitions became a song, caressing my people, gathering them to my heart. For indeed I loved them. 'My doctrine', I told them, 'shall drop as the rain, my speech shall distil as the dew; as the small rain upon the tender grass, and as the showers upon the herb.'

My vanity. Yet it would be so. This I knew. And now that vast congregation was silent, aware at last that their prophet was being removed from their midst; even, I told myself, thinking a little anxiously that they might need him in the troubled days to come.

Watching their upturned, serious faces, I chided myself for such thoughts. So, again, I sang to them, singing in a cracked old voice, singing about the love of God, singing about Jacob our ancestor.

'For the Lord's portion is his people.' This I instilled once more into their momentarily receptive hearts. 'Jacob is the lot of his inheritance. He found him in a desert land, and in the waste howling wilderness; he compassed him about, he cared for him, he kept him as the apple of his eye.'

And Jacob was my people, and my people were Jacob. They, too, the apple of the Lord.

'As an eagle that stirreth up her nest, that fluttereth over her young, he spread abroad his wings, he took them, he bare them on his pinions. The Lord alone did lead him and there was no strange god with him.'

I remembered the eagles of Horeb. I, even I, had been borne upon the wings of his compassion, covered in the feathers of his consolation.

'He made him ride on the high places of the earth, and he did eat the increase of the field; and he made him to suck honey out of the rock. . . .'

My voice rose and fell before the listening host, as I poured out my last warnings. Yes, warnings. But within myself I cried out. Why must it always be so? I would have spoken not of the arrows drunk with blood, but only of the everlasting arms, upholding. Yet both must be encompassed, and the light, as I had always known, was comprehended in the dark, as the dark was also a necessary part of the Lord's glory. From the beginning of time we had listened to the serpent, and, in our new-found knowledge, had not been strong enough always to choose the good. So I told them urgently to set their hearts upon the words I had spoken.

'For it is no vain thing for you; because it is your life, and through this thing ye shall prolong your days upon the land, whither ye go over Jordan to possess it.'

Then I blessed them, each tribe according to its own peculiar character, its own particular need. So many blessings, yet I had to remember them all, even though my remembrance was failing. I thought about my own desert journeys, the dryness and the silence and the endless yellow distance. So I said to them: 'Blessed of the Lord be his land, for the precious things of heaven, for the dew, and for the deep that coucheth beneath. . . .'

I remembered how the Sea of Reeds had drawn back to let us pass – the wet sand, the suffocating smell, the tide quaking and then withdrawing as a sucked-in breath, far down into the bed of the sea.

'And for the precious things of the fruits of the sun, and for the precious things of the growth of the moons, and for the chief things of the ancient mountains, and for the precious things of the everlasting hills.'

They were all there, the hot hard glare that yet would bless our fields, the moon waxing and waning above the night sky of the desert, the yellow ramparts of Horeb, the lesser stones of Hor, and the last climb into the harsh comforting of Nebo.

Now my people were chanting with me, surging about my chair, crying with tears of exultation and sorrow, and prostrating themselves upon the ground as a field whose stalks were bent by the desert wind.

'Hear, O Israel,' I sang with them, standing now, my arms uplifted over the kneeling host, 'the Lord our God is one Lord: and thou shalt love the Lord thy God with all thine heart, and with all thy soul, and with all thy might.'

It was Joshua who came, in the end, and led me away. Had he not always been there, from the beginning? Watchful over me. Always his hand ready, outstretched in love. Did I say in love? Yes, in love.

I stumbled a little, but he caught me. Yes, he had always been there. Underneath, I told myself, whimpering a little with age and weariness and pain and loss, are the everlasting arms, No, not Joshua's. The Lord God of Israel. My dwelling-place. The burning bush within which I had always been enclosed.

XXX

Come Now Therefore

They rested the litter several times along the steep track – Joshua and Caleb, Ithamar and Phinehas – not because they were exhausted but to spare me the jolting. In the blinding sunlight, even though sheltered by the woven canopy, I dozed against the cushions. I had not meant to sleep. It seemed a waste of my remaining time, eager as I was to look out – once – across the Promised Land. Yet, peering down at the serpent-twisting of the Jordan river, I found myself drifting, uncertain of the many figures about me. I even saw, or thought I saw, another figure, different from the rest, moving in majesty before me. Yet surely that could not be? For the malakh is come to announce the Lord, not to accompany his insignificant creation. But I seemed to see it. Or so I told myself. The old man, easily beguiled.

At times I know I murmured aloud, holding, it seemed, a conversation with the Lord. Had I not always done so? 'O Lord God,' I said, remembering this was only the start of our long journey, 'thou hast begun to show thy servant thy greatness, and thy strong hand, for what god is there in heaven or earth that can do according to thy words, and according to thy mighty acts?' Then, wheedling a little, though considering it to be unlikely, I added: 'Let me go over, I pray thee, and see the good land that is beyond Jordan. . . .'

But I knew the Lord had been wroth with me about this very question, and that he would not hearken. Indeed, immediately, there was his voice: 'Let it suffice thee; speak no more unto me of this matter. Get thee up into the top of Pisgah, and lift up thine eyes westward, and northward, and southward, and eastward, and behold with thine eyes: for thou shalt not go over this Jordan.'

I had known it. So I ceased my mumblings, and fixed my eyes upon the malakh. Or perhaps it was Joshua. I could no longer tell the difference.

Watching how the curtains of the litter shook to and fro, now concealing, now granting me glimpses of the sharp-stoned track, the dusty bushes, the lean goats moving indifferently out of our way, I thought that perhaps an old man's mind is rather like a curtain. Sometimes it is closed and everything within becomes woolly and stifled. Sometimes it is pulled open, so that a new awareness slants across the stuffy interior. I had noticed this in Aaron during his last days and, when I found it now in myself, the unwelcome confusion became suddenly informed by a moment of clarity.

Once I had walked easily to meet the Lord upon a mountain-top. Now, I had to be carried to meet him on yet another mountain. Once I had crouched at night beside my desert fire, asking my questions of the distant stars. Now, I hunched within my litter, avoiding the glare of the sun, my questions still unanswered. In the days before our exodus from Egypt, I had dwelt, it seemed, within a bubble of light, the ecstasy upon me, obedient to the Lord's loving commands and interpreting them to my people. Now, I was conscious that the ecstasy had diminished, worn thin perhaps by over-much exhortation and revealing rather more of stubborn displeasure, even anger, with which I had so often confronted the Lord's chosen.

In this I felt I had singularly resembled the Lord, dealing out his wrath, his chastisement, along with the holiness which was never mine. He had asked us to become holy – a terrible demand – and perhaps one day we might achieve this state. Meanwhile he would work through the limitations of our flesh: these small, inadequate yet chosen creatures being all the material that lay to his hand; knowing that, by our shortcomings, we turned him, always, into the victim of our imperfection. I, too, was his messenger, hampering him by my insufficiency.

And if the Lord had seen me as never entirely suitable, what had my people found in me? Sometimes, as I knew, they had thought me greater than I was. Had not the Lord said to me, speaking of Aaron: 'Thou shalt be to him as God'? There had been a danger for me, one which I had not always recognised.

But sometimes my people had thought of me quite differently.

— 185 —

What was it I had told them? The *Lord* hath sent me to do all these works; for I have not done them of mine own mind.' A defensive piece of self-justification it must have sounded, which hardly stood up to their experience of me. Uncertain of myself as I always had been, how then could I avoid an uneasy awareness of my people's uncertainty? Perhaps they had believed I was the prophet of my own ambition rather than the prophet of the Lord; even believing there had been no Voice on Mount Horeb – only my voice, spinning magic for them. I, the dreamer of dreams, deluded, and condemning them to years of hardship to satisfy my crazy visions.

I remembered warning them, long ago, against following false prophets, saying that such should be put to death. And? Had I not been stoned?

Here I made them halt the litter, and they withdrew from me while I thought these thoughts to their conclusion. Had I been only a dreamer of dreams? Had the whole story come out of my endless questioning as I had walked the wilderness? Had it just been my own voice, my own thoughts, my own capacity for ecstasy? Could I be certain, any more than my people, whether or not, on Mount Horeb, it had been the Lord's voice?

I climbed out of the litter then, knowing that I must make atonement, blind to the anxious looks and brushing aside the careful hands. I knelt beside the steep pathway, among my people but oblivious of them, pushing my ancient knees into the sharp stones, acknowledging my foolish vanity. So I refused, in the honest face of death, to see myself as other than I was: an indecisive man, cloven of tongue and cloven of mind. Yet chosen also. Prophet and leader and teacher. Had I been more than that? Bearer, perhaps, of the Lord's fire? Distributor of his holiness? Or but a thing puffed up?

Maybe it had seemed at times that I was God. Maybe it had seemed that there had been no God. I shrugged these speculations aside. The last enticement. The last vanity. To think myself God. To think there was no God. The two great temptations in the desert of the spirit.

No. I shook my head impatiently, flicking off such ideas as if they were the flies that buzzed tiresomely around me. Staring at nothing. Hearing the low whisper of voices, and knowing I was keeping them all waiting. Well, it was my death, surely? Prophet or prince, I should be ready in my own time. But I smiled, ruefully. In the Lord's time. After all, he would decide.

The mountainside was warm to my touch. The rock-walls reflected the heat in a shimmer of light which seemed like flame. The voices dissolved.

Put off thy shoes from off thy feet, he had said (and this I now did, kicking them from me), for the place whereon thou standest is holy ground. And no longer Mount Nebo, for I was back at my beginning, in the far desert before the burning bush. Moreover, he had said, I am the God of thy fathers, the God of Abraham, the God of Isaac, and the God of Jacob. I remembered that I had asked, Who am I? But he had not answered me, only replying, I shall be with thee. And, I shall be with thy mouth.

So I knelt upon Mount Nebo's stones yet also before the burning bush, repeating my question: 'Who am I? Who am I?'

I waited patiently, knowing the Lord was often ambiguous; knowing there might well be no answer.

But the answer came, and the Voice was gentle. 'Thou hast seen how that the Lord thy God bear thee, as a man doth bear his son.'

His son. I laid my head upon the ground and was silent. My heart was brimming with adoration. Adoration that was as fresh, as sharp, as piercing as when I had knelt before him for the first time.

And, just as it had happened then, the Voice now called me. 'Moses,' It cried, and again, 'Moses.'

What must I do? I went on kneeling there, my legs pressed into the hot stones, and I heard my own voice coming from a distant place, offering myself up to That which awaited me, offering the words once spoken.

'Here am I.'

After which, with much awkward stumbling, but irritably refusing all assistance, I climbed back into the litter, drawing the curtains close about me, uncertain where I might be. Yet the Voice came with me, calling, even as It had called in the wilderness.

'Come now therefore,' It adjured me. 'Come now therefore.'

Later, when we had reached the summit of Mount Nebo, a barren place, and I had looked into the Promised Land and had seen that impossible City shining in the dusky hills – seen also the Wall,

— 187 —

the holy Wall of Yerushalayim – I slept. Though perhaps it was not sleep.

I seemed to be once more in Horeb's golden, light-filled bowl. Only this time I lay upon the rock floor of the place, with the light pressing heavily and my body no longer an active part of me. Also, there were two men, standing one on each side of me, and though I could not move, I knew that there was war between them over my body. A rivalry as to which of them should bear me away. At this, I was divided by terror and longing, because I knew that one of these two men was the prince of demons, he who hinders; while the other was the prince of angels, he who is like unto God.

But the prince of demons is also known as the accuser, and I saw that his face was not evil, only tormented and dispossessed, a shadowed face inhabited by indecision, as if it were himself that he accused, so that, suddenly, I knew his face to be my own.

And the prince of angels, called also the guardian of Israel, the chief messenger of God, having a countenance of light through which the Lord's fire is to shine eternally, he also wore my face.

But they fought over me, and in the end I did not see which of them had borne me away.